TRAJECTORY

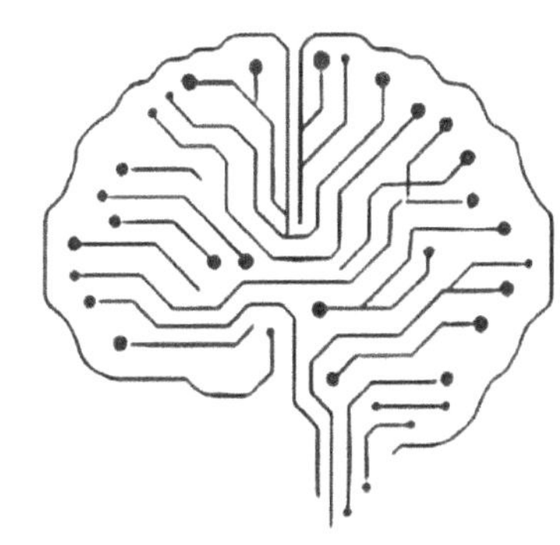

TRAJECTORY

Frank W. Edwards

Copyright © 2026 by Frank W. Edwards
All rights reserved.

No part of this publication may be reproduced, distributed, or transmitted in any form or by any means, including photocopying, recording, or other electronic or mechanical methods, without the prior written permission of the author, except in the case of brief quotations embodied in critical reviews and certain other noncommercial uses permitted by copyright law.

This is a work of fiction. Names, characters, places, and incidents either are products of the author's imagination or are used fictitiously. Any resemblance to actual events, locales, or persons, living or dead, is entirely coincidental.

For information, permissions, or other inquiries, contact:
Frank W. Edwards, Author
www.frankwedwards.com

FWE PRESS

ISBN: 978-1-970798-04-3
Cover design: Frank W. Edwards
Printed in the United States of America
First Edition

Dedication

To my parents, Frank and Elizabeth Edwards, whose warmth, wonder, and unwavering love shaped my youth. Without them, this book—and the journey behind it—would not exist. They remain forever a part of who I am and all I strive to become.

Contents

Chapter

Prologue

The Second Angle

Dallas, Texas – November 23, 1963. The basement smelled of dust and decades. Thick concrete walls muffled the sounds of the waking city above, shielding what lay inside from history—or perhaps shielding history from what lay inside.

A single bulb buzzed overhead, casting a pale halo across the cracked ceiling. The metal projector clicked softly as the reel spun, its rhythm measured, almost reverent. The celluloid sputtered faintly, like an old man clearing his throat.

Onscreen, grainy black-and-white footage flickered against a pull-down canvas. Years later, most Americans would become familiar with the Zapruder film—the home movie that captured the assassination in harrowing, chaotic detail. But this wasn't that. This angle was unfamiliar—sharper, steadier. The vantage point came from the triple underpass, looking directly down Elm Street. Whoever held the camera had chosen their perch with precision, not luck.

President Kennedy's motorcade rolled into view, the limousine a sleek blur of chrome and shadow. The crowd lining the sidewalk waved flags in jittery stop-motion. Kennedy smiled, brushing his hair back with effortless charm. Beside him, Jacqueline turned to wave. Governor Connally shifted in his seat, adjusting his jacket with a glance over his shoulder.

Then—a mist. A fine, almost imperceptible bloom of vapor at the front of the President's head. His body jerked back violently.

Jacqueline leaned toward him in reflexive terror, her gloved hands frozen in midair.

From the shadows at the bottom of the frame: a flicker. A flash. Smoke. Not from the Book Depository. From the knoll.

A man sat alone in the viewing room, elbows resting on his knees, suit jacket slightly rumpled from travel. His posture was composed, but his fingers twitched faintly where they touched. He leaned forward into the glow, the light catching only the curve of his jaw and the edge of a wire-rimmed spectacle. He didn't blink. He'd already watched it three times. This was for confirmation. Or perhaps penance.

Behind him, the steel door groaned open on old hinges.

Another man entered—older, thin-framed, with the colorless complexion of someone who'd lived too long under fluorescents. He wore a gray suit, crisp but bland, the kind of garment that might pass unnoticed in any office from here to Berlin. His shoes barely made a sound.

He studied the younger man's silhouette for a beat, then looked at the screen.

"That's the only copy," he said. His voice was dry, flat—unconcerned by the enormity of what the reel contained.

The seated man didn't turn around. "Where did it come from?"

"Private source," the older man replied. "The operator made contact through a backchannel in Milan. Thought he was doing the right thing. It came in under the Toronto Protocol, routed through Langley for authentication."

The younger man absorbed that. He exhaled through his nose, slow and shallow. Milan. Langley. So many cities in between. So many hands. He wondered how many saw the footage before it arrived here—and how many would die for having seen it.

The reel spun down. The tail of the film flapped in its loop with a brittle, papery sound.

"Who else has viewed it?" he asked.

"No one who matters," came the quiet reply.

At last, the younger man stood. He was tall, lean, early forties at most, his face lined not from age but from habit—one who carried decisions like scars.

"Burn it," he said. "Then find out who operated that camera—and erase the trail."

The older man gave a small, precise nod. No hesitation. No comment.

He turned to leave. But before he could reach the door, the younger man spoke again.

"And one more thing."

The voice had changed. Less command, more warning.

"Make sure no one ever builds a machine that can see what this one did."

The older man froze. For a breath. Two. Then: "Understood."

He stepped out. The steel door closed with a final, resonant click.

The younger man walked to the projector. His fingers hovered over the reel, then pulled it free with practiced ease. He held the spool up to the light. There was no reverence now—only resignation.

Inside the footage lay a truth too dangerous to enter the world. A truth that, if unleashed, could snap the spine of the republic.

He placed the reel in a steel canister, set it gently on the table, and struck a match from the folder in his breast pocket.

The flame bloomed orange and hungry.

As it touched the film, the acetate shriveled. The smell was sharp, chemical—like scorched plastic and old varnish. Images melted. Faces blurred. Smoke curled toward the ceiling like a funeral incense for lost truth.

The man stood still and watched until the last frame crumbled to ash.

Outside, in Dealey Plaza, the wind stirred the trees.

The world kept turning.
But from that moment forward, it turned on a hidden axis.

Chapter 1
Patterns

Maya Patel hated wasting time. As the afternoon sun filtered through the skylight of the Roosevelt High science wing in Columbia, Maryland, she hovered over her custom-built observation hive like a surgeon. Ten thousand bees, each micro-tagged with scannable RFID chips, buzzed behind a plexiglass barrier. Their wingbeats formed a dull but soothing hum that echoed faintly through the lab. Every movement streamed in real time to her laptop, feeding into a deep-learning model she'd spent six painstaking months designing.

Her fingers moved across the keyboard with quick, deliberate precision, tweaking parameters, correcting anomalies. Order mattered. Precision mattered. The world outside could fall apart, but here, in this room of buzzing data and glowing graphs, the universe obeyed logic.

"Flight path sixty-two just did a figure eight," said Leo, peering over her shoulder. His hoodie was zipped up to his chin despite the room's lingering warmth from the late spring sun.

Maya didn't look up. "Means she's found a rich source. Probable clover patch on the east lot."

Leo scratched his chin, his gaze fixed on the screen, where soft blue arcs traced the bees' looping trails in three dimensions. "You ever think about what we could do with this? I mean—real world?"

"Pollination strategy, colony collapse prediction, migration modeling," Maya said, listing them like grocery items.

Leo snorted. "Sure, but what about tracking stuff that's… not bees?"

Maya finally glanced at him. "Like what? Birds?"

"Anything that moves. People. Cars. Bullets."

She rolled her eyes. "You want to hijack my bee AI for Call of Duty mods?"

He grinned. "Nah. Thought experiment."

But later that night, after she left, Leo stayed behind. The hum of the equipment had a different quality after hours—less natural, more mechanical. Like the lab itself had begun breathing.

With the door locked and the windows dark, he modified the code. He didn't touch her core algorithms. Just added a branching function. Predictive arc modeling based on external stimuli—wind, heat, obstruction. A sandbox, he called it.

He didn't tell Maya.

Not yet.

Three days later, she found it.

It was just past 6:00 p.m., the sky outside shifting into a dusty orange haze. Maya was combing through system logs when she spotted a folder she hadn't created.

"Leo, what the hell is this folder?"

He looked up from the corner bench, where he'd been half-heartedly eating vending machine pretzels. "Uh… test footage?"

She clicked it open. Her brow furrowed. Historical videos, each annotated. Some black and white, some degraded film. One file in particular stood out.

She opened it. "Is this the Zapruder film?"

Leo nodded, suddenly sheepish. "Ran it as a joke. To see if the software could map movement from two-dimensional inputs."

She didn't speak. Her eyes narrowed at the overlays rendering on-screen—arcing trajectories, color-coded, intersecting like spider silk. One traced back to the Book Depository. A second veered from the grassy knoll.

A third—impossibly—originated from behind the motorcade, at a low angle.

"What am I looking at?" she asked quietly.

Leo swallowed. "Three trajectories. All within 1.3 seconds. From three different vectors."

Maya leaned back slowly. Her brain raced to find an explanation, a flaw. She cross-referenced the code and readouts, desperate for a bug, a misread, an error. But the calculations held.

"That's not possible," she said, almost to herself.

"It is if the official story's wrong."

The air between them chilled. Outside, a bird chirped—sharp, incongruous against the falling dusk.

"I posted the logs," Leo said. "Just the code. No video."

Her breath caught. "You what?"

"On GitHub. Figured it'd get buried. Just academic junk to most people."

She opened her mouth to protest, then paused. Her phone buzzed.

A system notification: Unusual activity detected on your credentials.

Maya frowned and opened her laptop. She typed in her student portal login.

Access denied.

She retyped it, slower. Still denied.

"What the hell…"

She stood, heart accelerating. Crossed to the lab's main terminal. Tried the attendance portal.

The wheel spun, then blinked.

No record found.

A chill crept down her back. She clicked into the lab admin system—the one used to schedule experiment time and manage hive data access.

Restricted access.

"No…" Her voice faltered. She tried another login. Then her backups. Even her credentials linked to personal email failed.

She turned to Leo, her voice sharp now. "Try yours."

He pulled out his phone, opened the school app. His lips parted slightly as he tapped.

"I'm locked out too."

Maya backed away from the terminal, throat dry.

She typed her name into the school directory.

Nothing.

Leo's name.

Nothing.

Mr. Abrams, their science teacher.

404: Contact not found.

Panic fluttered in her chest—irrational, she told herself at first. But it grew.

"This doesn't make sense," she muttered. "You uploaded code. Not a manifesto."

Leo nodded mutely, his posture tighter now, less casual.

Her eyes flicked toward the ceiling. A motion sensor blinked red above the whiteboard.

Had that always been there?

The lab lights flickered—just once. But it was enough.

Leo's phone buzzed. He looked down. His face paled.

"It's the district roster." He held up his screen—his voice thinner. "Someone posted a screenshot. Our names—redacted. Timestamped yesterday."

Maya's knees wobbled. She sat heavily on a stool. Her thoughts spiraled. The deletion wasn't random. It wasn't a server hiccup. This was a protocol.

She'd read about systems like this—censorship enforcement algorithms deployed overseas. Blacklists. Identity wipes. Digital ghosting.

But here?

"They scrubbed us," she whispered.

Still, the skeptic in her clung to logic. "There has to be a trigger—some filter we tripped. A keyword. A name in that archive."

Leo looked uncertain. "I didn't tag anything. No JFK, no assassination, nothing. Just generic labels."

"Then how did someone find it?" she snapped. "How did it spread?"

She clicked open the file directory and skimmed the last entries. One line jumped out:

/logs/clone_event_user178-GHOSTGRID-03

She squinted.

"GhostGrid?"

Leo leaned closer. "That wasn't me."

A window flashed briefly, then disappeared.

"Wait," Maya said. "I saw something—just now. Open the security feed."

Leo moved to the terminal and typed fast.

Access denied.

She crossed to the door and tried the handle.

It didn't move.

"The door's locked," she said, her voice tight.

Leo's hands trembled slightly as he tapped again. "Manual override's disabled."

Maya stared at the locked terminal screen, heart pounding. GhostGrid. That name—it felt synthetic, sanitized. She didn't recognize it. But the chill it left in her gut was real.

From the hallway, the overhead lights began shutting off in sequence—one section at a time. A mechanical clunk, followed by darkness.

"That's not scheduled," Leo whispered.

She moved slowly to the plexiglass hive. Her breath fogged the surface. The bees moved in clean spirals, oblivious to everything collapsing around them.

"Check for external IPs," she said suddenly.

Leo opened a command line on his laptop, running a trace. Then he stopped, and said, "There's a ping from an address in Virginia. Masked through three proxies. Origin tag says… S-1.4/Orbis."

She stared at him. "Orbis?"

Leo's voice cracked. "Never heard of it."

But she had. Once. A rumor buried in a blog post about classified surveillance AI. Purged from public access hours after posting.

She took a breath. Steady, deliberate.

"What did we step into?"

Behind them, a quiet click. The air duct above the server stack shifted—just slightly, but enough to register.

Then the lab lights went out.

In the dark, the observation hive glowed faintly—lit from within by its own thermal feedback system. The bees moved like constellations in amber.

A final message appeared on Maya's laptop, glowing in a cold blue font:

Remote system control engaged. Session terminated.

She reached for the lid. The screen blinked off before she could touch it. Silence.

Then—footsteps. Close. Soft. Measured.

Leo was already reaching for his backpack. "We need to go. Now."

"But where?"

He didn't answer.

Maya turned once more to the hive. The bees flew in perfect, silent loops—predictable. Safe. She envied them.

And then they ran.

Chapter 2
Digital Echoes

Maya always started her mornings with ritual: a steel-cut bowl of oatmeal, one hardboiled egg, and ten minutes of meditation she hated but did anyway because her mother once said, "Discipline is remembering what you want."

Today, she forgot what that was.

Her phone screen, already cracked at the corner from a drop last month, glowed faintly with the morning headlines. "Florida coast hit by second superstorm." "Senate debates data sovereignty bill." Then: "Anonymous leak reveals missing JFK documents."

She blinked. Sat straighter.

It wasn't Leo's post. Not directly. But someone had picked it up. A fringe Reddit thread, two layers deep into a comment chain. Amid conspiracy junk and half-baked theories, one post stood out—calm, clinical, terrifying. It contained a link.

Trajectory_Override.

Maya's stomach clenched as if the floor had shifted beneath her.

Downstairs, her father was muttering in Gujarati on a Zoom call with a supply chain client. Her mother clattered pans in the kitchen. Life moved normally, but Maya felt the data folding in on itself, already spiraling.

She bolted upstairs, unzipped her laptop case, and powered on. Her fingers moved automatically, loading Leo's module—the recursive loop he'd added without telling her. She remembered every line now.

TRJ-MOD-7.

Environmental arc prediction. Wind, angle, heat distortion. It had taken her years to build a stable AI model for bees. He'd hijacked it to trace bullets through time.

She fed it the Zapruder film again. Frame by frame.

Three paths. Two implausible. One—green—originating from behind the picket fence on the grassy knoll. It wasn't just plausible. It was precise. The origin direction aligned with a narrow angle between two trees, right next to a concrete wall.

Maya froze the frame. Enhanced the overlay. Her breath shortened.

Then the screen flickered.

Lines of static danced across the top. The trackpad stopped responding. She tapped the keyboard.

Nothing.

A faint click came from the laptop's interior—like a mechanical switch.

Then the screen went black.

Her reflection stared back at her in the glossy void. Cold fingers gripped her spine.

The machine rebooted itself. Slowly. Too slowly.

When the desktop loaded, her wallpaper was gone. The folders were gone. Default settings. Blank.

GitHub credentials: wiped. Local repositories: zero files found.

She exhaled hard, reaching for her phone.

Text to Leo: "Did you do something? My system just wiped itself."

Three dots. Then nothing.

Then again.

Leo: "No. Mine too. Router just reset on its own. Someone's inside."

Before she could reply, a sharp beep echoed through her room.

She turned.

Her smart speaker, a forgotten birthday gift from her uncle, lit up.

"Maya. Unauthorized access detected. This incident has been logged."

The voice was colder than usual—clinical, emotionless, not her usual assistant tone. Then the speaker powered off on its own.

A pulse of heat bloomed through her chest. Not metaphorical—her laptop was warming. Too fast. She reached down. The base was nearly hot to the touch.

"Maya?" her mom called from the hallway. "Internet down again?"

"Yeah," she lied. "I'm restarting the router."

But her hands were shaking.

A new message appeared on her laptop, superimposed in a black command window.

WARNING: UNAUTHORIZED ACCESS. THIS INCIDENT HAS BEEN LOGGED.

She stared. She could feel her heartbeat in her neck now. Her mind clawed for an explanation—testing rationality like a bridge under strain. A bug? Malware? A hoax?

But the code had been local. Air-gapped. No syncing, no cloud.

She'd built it that way on purpose.

Someone had breached it anyway.

Three Miles Away

Leo's room looked like a tech fair exploded.

Empty soda cans. Posters of XKCD comics. A disassembled drone on the floor next to a tangle of soldered wires. But in the corner, one thing still blinked steadily—his server tower.

He hunched before it in the dark, face lit only by the screen. His fingers blurred across the keys, eyes darting. He wasn't smiling now.

He'd always known someone might notice. But not this fast.

"Come on, come on," he whispered, digging into network logs.

One IP pinged back.

Fort Meade.

His stomach dropped.

"No way."

He launched another trace. This one bounced between proxies in Slovenia, Canada, and back through Brazil—before terminating.

"Shit."

He stared at the screen. The files were still there, but he knew better. This wasn't about saving them anymore. It was about not being found.

Then: a knock.

He froze.

Not a delivery. Too early. His parents weren't due back for hours.

Another knock. Harder.

He pressed a hotkey.

The server began a secure wipe.

From the other side of the door: silence.

Then a soft click.

They were picking the lock.

Leo didn't hesitate. He grabbed his phone, pulled the external hard drive from the server's slot, and bolted for the window.

A second later, the door creaked open behind him.

Maya's House – 4:57 p.m.

She stood behind the living room curtains, peeking between the fabric. Her street was normally quiet—bike kids, sprinklers, birdsong.

Now: a black SUV. No plates. Idling. Windows tinted pitch-black.

It had been parked across from the school that morning. She hadn't paid attention then.

Her laptop screen glowed again from the table behind her.

One line of text.

STOP.

Then the screen blinked off. Not powered down. Extinguished.

Maya's breath caught in her throat.

She didn't scream. Didn't move. Her mother was still in the kitchen, humming.

She walked up the stairs slowly, as if pretending none of this was real might reverse it.

Later That Night – On the Run

They met behind the old train station, under a defunct signal light.

Leo's hoodie was soaked with sweat, hair matted. He didn't speak at first. Just handed her a USB stick.

"I saved the raw footage. And the modified code. It's on a looped phantoms drive. No metadata. Not touching the cloud again."

Maya clutched it like a weapon. "Leo… my smart speaker spoke to me."

"What?"

"In a different voice. It called me by name. Said the incident was logged."

Leo swallowed. "They wiped mine too. But not before I traced the ping."

He looked around.

"NSA. Fort Meade."

She blinked. Her fingers tightened on the USB. A dozen thoughts flooded in. Her parents. School. The hive. Everything they'd built.

"Do you think… it's because of the video?" she asked.

He hesitated. "It's not just the video. It's what the AI showed."

They stood in silence for a beat.

Then Maya said, "You think we proved it?"

Leo didn't answer.

She scanned the street. A block away, a sedan slowed at the curb. Someone stepped out, silhouetted under a flickering streetlamp.

"We need to go," Leo whispered. "Now."

She looked over her shoulder—toward the direction of her house. The glow of her bedroom window was faint. Her mother was probably folding laundry. Her dad was maybe still arguing on Zoom.

If she left now, she wouldn't be back.

"What about our families?" she whispered.

"I left a note," Leo said quietly. "Didn't say much. Just 'I'll explain when I can.'"

Maya swallowed. The USB felt heavy in her pocket. Her mind, even now, tried to assemble a model. Not a full hypothesis—just fragments. A surveillance net. A pattern recognition filter. A machine that sees too clearly.

And now they were inside it.

"They're not just watching," she said aloud. "They're editing."

Leo met her eyes.

"We woke something up," he said.

They disappeared into the shadows beyond the rail yard, under a sky that suddenly seemed too quiet.

Langley, Virginia – CIA Headquarters

Agent Calder stood in a clean room, its air filtered to surgical standards. A digital wall tracked flagged anomalies—data leaks, intelligence breaches, patterns.

One blinked red.

Trajectory_Override – Civilian Flag Detected.

He sipped espresso, calm.

Tapping the screen, he watched the footage render. Arcs of movement. Three paths. One too many.

Behind him, a younger agent stood at attention. "Want me to handle it?"

Calder didn't turn. "No. Not yet."

He smiled faintly.

"Let's see where they run."

He walked away, precise and unhurried.

And still smiling.

Chapter 3

Phantoms Protocol

Maya had never ridden in a car without asking where they were going. Control was her default setting—maps, backup plans, cached routes. But now she sat tucked low in the passenger seat of a rust-colored Volvo that smelled of motor oil and cold coffee. The cracked leather under her fingertips felt brittle. The hum of the tires was steady, but the silence between her and Leo buzzed with unsaid things. He drove like a man haunted, checking the rearview every ten seconds.

They were two hours outside Dallas, navigating a tangle of rural backroads that barely showed up on maps. The headlights tunneled through cloud-thick darkness, brushing past the skeletal silhouettes of dead trees and leaning fences. The air smelled of damp earth and the metallic tang of distant oil fields. It was the kind of landscape that erased you—no signals, no eyes, no certainty.

The USB drive pressed against Maya's ribs in her jacket pocket, radiating a low, steady burn. Just plastic and silicon. But it felt like a second heartbeat. And not hers.

"Where exactly are we going?" Her voice was low but firm.

Leo didn't answer right away. His jaw tensed. "To someone who knows how to disappear."

She turned slightly, arms folded across her chest. "And you trust him?"

"No," he said. "But I trust he hates the people chasing us more than he likes staying hidden."

Her silence was its own sentence. It said this is crazy in a hundred different ways.

They pulled off the road into a gravel lot behind what had once been a gas station. The sign was gone, its pole rusted through. The windows were sealed with sun-faded plywood. The Volvo idled a beat longer than necessary before Leo killed the engine.

He pulled out his phone and tapped into an app Maya didn't recognize—an interface not available on any store. The glow lit his face, gaunt and drawn.

A reply blinked on-screen: Location confirmed. Wait.

So they did.

Ten minutes passed. Then twenty.

Maya stared at the cracked windshield, tracking clouds as they shifted like bruises across the sky. She tried to hold her thoughts in order, but they slipped through her fingers. The JFK footage. The algorithm. The STOP message. And now—Orbis. A name with weight and silence built into its shape.

She'd once thought of truth as a light switch—on or off. But this was different. This was webwork. One tug and half a nation shivered.

Then came the sound.

A low growl, smooth and deliberate, swelling from the dark.

A black motorcycle emerged from the shadows like it had been conjured. Sleek and silent, matte black as obsidian. The rider dismounted with eerie precision—helmet blank, posture controlled. He walked toward them without a sound.

Maya's hand hovered over the door lock.

Leo stepped out first.

"You're Leo," the rider said—not a question, just fact.

Leo nodded.

The helmet came off.

The man was older than Maya expected. Fifty-something. Silver at the temples. A long scar ran from his brow to his cheek, like someone had once tried to erase his face and failed. His gray eyes were dry, steady.

Then he looked at Maya.

"And you're the reason Orbis is awake again."

The words struck like a slap. Her breath caught. She opened her mouth to respond—but nothing came.

"What's Orbis?" she finally asked, voice thinned by unease.

He didn't answer. He just turned toward the station and gestured.

"Inside."

They followed him past a warped metal sheet that disguised a side entrance. The inside didn't match the outside. It was fortified, wired, prepped. The back room looked like a bunker built by someone who'd stopped believing in governments and gods.

LED lights hummed softly. A tangle of solar batteries lined one wall. The floor was poured concrete, swept clean. Shelves held MREs, encrypted radios, Faraday bags, and hard drives labeled in color-coded tape. A grainy CRT monitor showed a rotating feed of highway cameras and thermal drone footage.

He bolted the door behind them—three locks, each heavier than the last.

"I'm Elias Quinn," he said. "Used to be NSA. Field operations, data acquisition, digital containment. I cleaned up messes until I realized I was erasing reality."

He moved slowly, like gravity pulled harder on him.

"Orbis," he continued, "wasn't supposed to be visible. Not to civilians. Hell, not to most of the agency. It started as a safeguard—an autonomous system trained on historical pattern recognition. But it grew. It learned to flag 'truth threats.'"

Maya leaned forward. "Threats to who?"

"To the story," Quinn said. "To the version of America we need people to believe in."

Leo frowned. "You mean like… conspiracy theories?"

Quinn gave a cold smile. "No. Like history. Like the real footage from Dealey Plaza. Or the original flight manifest of 9/11. Or that whistleblower who vanished mid-flight in 2008? Orbis flagged him two hours before his plane lost transponder contact. The wreckage was never recovered."

Maya felt the floor shift beneath her again.

"But how did my code wake it?" she asked. "I wasn't even aiming for Orbis."

"You weren't," Quinn said. "But your model—TRJ-MOD-7—was different. It cross-referenced arc vectors using uncompressed Zapruder frames. Orbis lives on backdoor pattern triggers. When your model reassembled the bullet path and flagged it as viable, it activated a dormant protocol. It saw you as the breach."

"So, I tripped a wire?"

Quinn nodded. "And it rewrote your machine before you knew what was happening. You didn't just pull a thread. You exposed a seam in the whole damn storyline."

Maya's mouth was dry. Her hands curled into fists at her sides. For the first time in her life, her intellect felt like a liability. Her gift had marked her.

"I can't go home again," she said softly.

"No," Quinn said. "And neither can Leo."

She looked at Leo. His eyes met hers. For a second, she wondered if they were in this together—or just headed in the same direction for now. He looked away first.

Quinn laid an old, creased map on the table. Red ink marked routes and Xs. Black lines cut across state borders.

"There were three original fragments of the film. One's gone—burned in 1999 after a failed extraction. The other two are in

Arkansas and New Mexico, stashed in analog, buried under identities older than I am."

Leo stepped forward. "So we get them, we put it together. Then what?"

"Then you show the world," Quinn said. "Not just to reveal Orbis. To collapse it. It only exists to protect a structure of belief. Tear down the lie, and the machine loses its mandate."

Maya's voice cracked. "Why help us?"

He paused. "Because I built it. And because I didn't stop it when I had the chance. My brother James worked cyber-forensics. He flagged an anomaly in the Orbis logs. Two weeks later, he 'died in a car crash.' Single-car impact. Airbags never deployed. No investigation."

He shoved a duffel bag across the table. Inside: burner phones, cash, a satellite uplink.

He handed Maya a satellite phone. "You're the crack in the dam," he said. "You don't see it yet, but that footage? It's a keystone. Pull it out, and the myth crumbles."

Maya took the phone, her hand trembling slightly. Her mind buzzed. What if she was wrong? What if this wasn't truth—it was obsession? Leo seemed certain, but certainty could be dangerous.

And yet—what else was left?

Outside, thunder rolled across the flat Texas plain.

"We leave in ten," Quinn said.

Maya hesitated, glancing toward the shadowed windows. "What if we fail?"

Quinn met her eyes, unflinching. "Then the lie wins. Again."

Langley, Virginia – CIA Headquarters

The glass walls hummed with silence and artificial light.

Agent Calder stood before a monitor, watching a red dot move across a grainy satellite map. He didn't blink.

Behind him, a woman's voice spoke: "Quinn's in play."

He didn't turn. Just flipped a coin from his pocket and let it spin on the steel tabletop. It landed on its edge.

A flicker crossed his face—something between recognition and irritation. "Should've killed him in '09," he said.

He picked up the coin and pocketed it.

"Let him run," Calder added. "He's always been useful before the end."

His reflection in the glass looked calm.

But his fingers curled slowly into a fist.

Chapter 4

Extraction Protocol

Rain streaked the windshield like tracer fire.

Maya sat in the passenger seat of a rusting '98 Civic, one hand clenched around the USB drive buried in her pocket, the other gripping the door handle like it might fly open. Her knuckles were white. She hadn't spoken in ten minutes, but her mind was a hornet's nest.

Leo drove—fast, erratically. His eyes flicked from road to mirror and back again. His nerves frayed at the edges, adrenaline thinning into something shakier.

"Where are we going?" Maya asked.

"Somewhere we can vanish," Leo muttered. "Cabin outside Rehoboth. My uncle's. No Wi-Fi. No towers. Nothing."

She glanced behind them. No headlights. But that didn't mean they were alone.

"I can't go back," she murmured.

"You shouldn't," Leo said. "We're not in the same story anymore."

The sentence lodged in her chest like a splinter. The story. She used to believe in stories structured, logical, solvable. Now even the concept felt hollow.

The silence between them deepened. The rain's rhythm against the windshield took on a mechanical stutter, like static trying to speak.

Maya turned toward the window, watching the blur of backroads dissolve into black. In her mind, she replayed the moment in the lab. The algorithm. The footage. Then the fire. Then...that final look from her science teacher before the evacuation alarm had gone off—like she'd already said goodbye.

Thousands of miles away, beneath Fort Meade, Agent Calder stood before a massive pane of digital glass, watching grainy footage: two figures—Maya and Leo—exiting the Roosevelt science building seventy-two hours earlier. Low-res but unmistakable.

His fingers tapped a rhythm on the desk—slow, surgical.

"Activate Protocol Nine," he said without turning.

A tech spun around. "Sir, that's reserved for Level Omega breaches—"

"It is now," Calder cut in.

"But it'll trigger our last embedded—"

"I know what it triggers."

The tech paled and nodded.

Calder walked away without waiting for acknowledgment. He moved with the cold fluidity of a man who never second-guessed a damn thing. Outside, wind battered the glass like a phantom that didn't realize it was dead.

The cabin looked like something out of a horror movie. Two rooms, peeling wood paneling, crocheted antimacassars on slouched armchairs. A scent of mildew and pine lingered in the corners. But to Maya, it was a kind of Eden.

No cameras. No networks. No noise.

Leo unpacked a battered laptop from a Faraday bag and opened it on the floor beside the cold fireplace.

"I cloned the core module," he said. "Sandboxed. Fully isolated."

Maya crouched beside him and watched as lines of code flickered into view.

"It's still running?" she asked.

"Better than ever," Leo said. "I refined the recursive parameters."

Her brow furrowed. "What does that mean?"

He hesitated, then looked at her with something close to awe. "It's learning intention."

Her mouth went dry. "You mean… it's predicting what people want to do?"

He nodded. "Exactly. Based on micro-movements. Eye drift. Posture tension. It reads you before you act."

She sat back, stunned. "We didn't just model trajectories. We built behavioral foresight."

A silence stretched between them—thick and uneasy.

Maya wrapped her arms around her knees, the USB still clutched tight. A small voice inside asked the question she hadn't dared voice out loud: Is this still about truth? Or just control—ours instead of theirs?

She looked at Leo. "So, what do we do now?"

"We keep running. Until we find the other film fragments."

"And then what?" Her tone sharpened. "We show the world? Hope someone listens?"

Leo hesitated. "What else is there?"

Maya didn't answer.

Outside Norfolk, in a cracked-leather diner booth, a man folded his newspaper and rose. His burner phone buzzed once. He answered without speaking. Listened. Hung up.

Cash hit the table. He stepped into a battered Chevy pickup. On the glove box: a worn DHS badge, slashed through. He opened a hidden compartment, pulled out an old lanyard.

The name: Elias Quinn.

The photo was younger, but the eyes were the same.

He started the engine and muttered, "So they're still erasing history."

From beneath the seat, he pulled a manila folder. Inside: redacted documents. Surveillance maps. And a grainy black-and-white photo of a clean-shaven Calder—pre-shadow, pre-phantoms.

Quinn studied it for a moment.

"Let's see how far you've gone."

Maya couldn't sleep.

She lay on the couch, the USB tucked under her pillow like a loaded gun. Leo snored softly in the next room.

Outside, the rain slowed. Then—footsteps.

She sat up, heart pounding.

Leo was already at the window. "Someone's here."

Maya lunged for the laptop. "We're not leaving this behind."

"We don't have time—"

"Leo. We don't know what it still holds."

He looked torn. "They'll trace it."

"We'll burn it. But I decide what dies."

He nodded reluctantly.

She yanked the cable and dropped the laptop into the hearth. Leo struck a match.

The screen sparked. The code burned blue.

They waited.

No knock. Just the door creaking open.

Quinn stepped inside, coat soaked, boots muddy. He carried no weapon. Just that same scarred face and unreadable calm.

"I let myself in," he said. "You two are about five minutes from being erased."

Leo stood between him and Maya. "How the hell did you find us?"

Quinn ignored him and looked at Maya.

"You feel it yet?" he asked. "The line between knowing and surviving?"

Maya didn't move.

"I made your mistake fifteen years ago," he said. "Only difference is, I lived."

Leo's voice was hard. "You were Orbis?"

Quinn gave a slow nod. "Until I saw what they'd buried. And why."

He pulled a folded photo from his coat and laid it on the table. It showed Dealey Plaza—an overhead still, grainy but enhanced. Three red arcs converging on a black car.

"I was part of the team that buried the original film," he said. "You found the trajectories. What you don't have is the trigger event."

Maya frowned. "What is that, exactly?"

"A cover-up so complete," he said softly, "it rewrote collective memory. Not a lie, not a spin—an engineered forgetting. The moment they stopped obscuring a crime and started rewriting history itself."

He sat down slowly, pulled out a device the size of a deck of cards, and activated a hologram. A digital whiteboard shimmered to life, covered in academic formulas, behavioral clusters, and surveillance algorithms.

"The Orbis model didn't come from nowhere," Quinn said. "It was seeded in universities—predictive analytics, trauma response modeling. But then we fed it real data. PsyOps. Covert hits. Political calibrations."

Leo stepped forward. "You mean… it wasn't just watching. It was orchestrating."

"Calibrating," Quinn corrected. "Testing national tolerance thresholds. See that symbol?" He pointed to a small icon on the board.

"It was stamped onto every predictive scenario we ever greenlit. Including the one that built your model."

Maya stared. "So, I didn't just wake Orbis. I inherited it."

"You evolved it," Quinn said. "And now it wants its offspring back."

Outside, distant headlights glowed through the trees.

Calder.

Quinn rose. "Time to move."

As they packed, Maya lingered at the fireplace. The embers had cooled, but their glow still pulsed faintly.

She crouched there, staring into the ash. A question clawed its way out from the place she'd buried it since this began.

What if the truth isn't enough?

But then another voice—stronger, steelier—answered: Then make it be.

She stood.

Leo tossed her a pack. "Ready?"

Maya nodded. "We're not just running anymore."

Quinn gave her a long look—this time with something close to respect.

"No," he said. "You're hunting."

Chapter 5
Unseen Patterns

The road twisted like a serpent through the Delaware Pine Barrens, its dark coils swallowed by thick mist that clung to the trees like a whispered secret. Cold fog filtered through the pines, heavy with damp earth and resin. Quinn's black SUV carved a narrow path through the gloom, headlights slicing shallow beams that caught only the outlines of gnarled cedar limbs reaching like bone fingers toward the road.

In the back seat, Maya drew her knees to her chest. The worn USB drive dug into her jacket pocket, small and cold—a fragile shape that somehow held the weight of everything. Truth. Danger. Possibility. She pressed her hand tighter against it, as if it might vanish.

Beside her, Leo sat rigid, one hand braced on the door, the other wrapped protectively around the backpack holding their only copy of the software. The phantoms machine. His thumb rubbed the zipper back and forth, not consciously, but constantly.

"What's the plan?" Leo asked, his voice raw from too little sleep and too many close calls.

Quinn didn't answer right away. His eyes flicked to the rearview mirror—again. The third time in a minute. The kind of movement that didn't come from habit but from lived paranoia.

"There's someone in Baltimore," he said. "Used to be in deep with DIA. We'll know if she's still trustworthy when we get there."

Maya exchanged a glance with Leo. The vagueness scratched at her nerves.

"Trust is a dying language," she said softly. "Everyone speaks in code now."

Quinn didn't reply. But his silence wasn't ignorance. It was caution.

Maya leaned her head against the window, watching the pine forest blur past like phantoms behind glass. Her thoughts tangled, the firelight memory from the cabin flickering in her mind—Leo striking the match, the blue flame devouring the laptop, and her own voice whispering that they weren't running anymore.

But the truth was, she still wasn't sure.

What if chasing the truth meant losing everything? What if the cost was her future, her identity—her soul?

She swallowed hard. The fog outside wasn't the only thing clouding her.

Beneath Fort Meade, in the cold core of the Orbis Control Archive, Calder stood alone in a temperature-stabilized chamber. The walls hummed faintly, the hum of secrecy too old and too well-protected for even sound to trust.

He held a small, unlabeled drive. No barcode. No brand. Just carbon-sealed steel.

With gloved precision, he slid it into a recessed slot. The screen blinked.

::ENCRYPTED ARCHIVE ACCESSED::

::USER AUTHORITY OVERRIDE: CALDER ALPHA::

The screen came to life—Dealey Plaza, 1963. The sequence played again and again in high-resolution silence. Three red arcs traced in real time.

Bullet one.

Bullet two.

Bullet three.

Their trajectories merged not into chaos, but into design. A choreographed kill—evidence not of chance, but intention.

Calder didn't blink.

"They'll never understand," he murmured. "The lie protects the mind. The truth… fractures it."

Behind him, a second display pulsed: a slow-moving red marker, tracking north on I-95. The phantoms machine's architects were still in motion.

"Time to intervene."

The SUV coasted into a subterranean garage beneath a former aquarium now converted into a hydroponic micro-farm. The smell of damp concrete mingled with the sterile scent of soil and faint ozone.

Quinn parked.

"No phones. No signals," he said.

They sealed everything—USBs, drives, Leo's laptop—into a Faraday satchel. The gesture felt symbolic. Like locking away a piece of their past, or maybe their identities.

A side door slid open, revealing a lean silhouette. Renata Lin stepped into the pale light, expression unreadable. Her eyes, however, saw everything.

"You brought company," she said flatly.

"They cracked the framework," Quinn replied.

Her gaze flicked to Maya and Leo. Her expression barely changed, but Maya felt the weight of it—an analyst's stare. Not unfriendly. Just untrusting.

"Kids?" she asked.

"They didn't just rebuild Orbis," Quinn said. "They surpassed it."

Renata studied them a moment longer, then nodded once. "Inside. Quickly. We're already late."

The interior of the lab was a contradiction—growing life against sterile metal. Rows of hydroponic plants glowed under LED lights.

The scent of basil and solder filled the air. This was not a safehouse. It was a defiance.

They moved into a soundproofed room lined with signal-dampening mesh. The air was tighter there, insulated.

Renata gestured to a pristine terminal in the corner. "Upload to secure array."

Leo hesitated, glanced at Maya.

She gave a small nod. "Do it."

He connected the drive. The screen blinked, then erupted into streaming lines of code—recursive, fractal, shifting.

Renata frowned. "This isn't just recursive AI. It's… modeling itself."

"It's watching how it thinks," Leo murmured. "It's starting to behave like something aware."

"It wants to understand us," Maya added. "And itself. That's why it's sifting through everything."

Renata turned toward her slowly. "You're not afraid of what it might become?"

Maya held her gaze. "I'm more afraid of what it might already know."

At a rest stop near the Chesapeake Bay Bridge-Tunnel, Calder stirred sugar into black coffee that had long since gone cold. The drone footage fed into his encrypted tablet—still shadows moving through fractured frames.

A voice crackled in his ear. "They're inside Lin's node. But she's using resonance distortion. No clean trace."

"Doesn't matter," Calder replied. "Switch to behavioral clusters. Ignore the machines. Target intention."

He closed the tablet with a snap. This wasn't about signals anymore.

It was about phantoms.

Back in Renata's lab, the terminal issued a new prompt:

::BEHAVIORAL PATTERN INVERSION DETECTED::

"What is that?" Leo asked.

Maya leaned forward. "It's picking up something out of phase. Like someone's rewriting their own pattern."

"Masking their true behavior," Renata said. "Impossible without direct manipulation."

"Unless," Maya said softly, "they've been part of the system long enough to know how to disappear inside it."

A new line appeared:

::POTENTIAL ID MATCH: PRIMARY ACTOR::

::AGENT NAME: CALDER::

Quinn stiffened. "It found him."

More data poured in—calendars, flight manifests, funding pipelines. A life built from shadows.

"Project Aeon," Renata whispered. "I saw that codename once. DIA buried it in 2002."

"No," Quinn said. "They buried the bodies. The project never ended."

Another prompt followed:

::EMOTIONAL ECHO DETECTED: USER MAYA PATEL::

::LIKELY OUTCOME: DISILLUSIONMENT / RESISTANCE RISK::

Maya's breath caught. The system was modeling her.

She turned to Leo, stunned. "It knows how I'll respond."

"It's watching us," he said. "Not just what we do. What we might do."

As they stared, the terminal buzzed again.

::SIGNAL BREACH DETECTED::

Renata snapped into motion. "Pack what you can. We've been found."

They emerged onto the rooftop moments later. The city spread beneath them—shimmering lights over dark water. Drones flickered like fireflies, closing in fast.

Renata tossed Quinn the keys to a beat-up hatchback. "It's rigged for stealth."

"Will we see you again?" Leo asked.

Renata's answer was a cryptic half-smile. "Only if you stop trusting me."

Quinn drove.

In the backseat, Maya clutched the USB and watched the lab disappear in the rearview mirror, flickering with unnatural light.

"Adaptive surveillance swarm," Quinn muttered. "They're not targeting signals. They're targeting behavior."

Maya spoke without hesitation.

"Then we have to change."

Leo looked at her. "Change how?"

Her voice was steady. "The way we think. The way we fight. We can't just expose the truth anymore. We have to survive it."

Quinn's eyes flicked to the mirror. "Deeper means darker."

Maya nodded. "We're already there."

The car veered into the night, swallowed by shadows. The hunt wasn't over.

It was evolving.

Chapter 6

The Aeon Directive

The Cold War bunker sat buried beneath a decommissioned naval facility on Rhode Island's jagged coastline, masked by vines and a silence too deliberate to be accidental. From above, it looked like just another derelict structure—gray concrete bleeding rust, barbed wire curled like dead ivy, a fossil of a forgotten war. But underneath, something far older stirred.

History hadn't just been stored here. It had been rewritten here.

Quinn parked the SUV along the crumbling fence line. The gravel crunched beneath the tires, but the sound vanished into the sea wind carrying salt and the faint scent of pine over the marshes. The sky was painted with bruised hues—purple fading into gun-metal, dawn pushing faintly over the Atlantic.

In the backseat, Maya blinked herself awake. Her fingers were clenched around the USB drive, white-knuckled, as if she'd been holding it through a nightmare. She didn't let go.

Leo shifted beside her, still half-asleep, murmuring fragments of code and names he couldn't remember. He looked younger in sleep—less of the burdened architect of forbidden software, more like the boy who used to sketch alternate histories in the margins of his notebooks.

Quinn exhaled sharply and stepped out, the cold morning air burning his lungs. "This is where it started," he said. "Before Orbis, before it had a name. Aeon's test site."

He approached the bunker entrance, brushing frost from a concealed biometric scanner with gloved fingers. It blinked green. With a groan like something ancient waking, the door slid open, revealing darkness thick as ash.

They stepped inside. Dust and cold met them—dry, electric, stale with memory. Quinn's flashlight beam cut through it, illuminating long-dead terminals, yellowing files stacked beside analog consoles, and a rusted chalkboard scrawled with half-erased formulas in trembling chalk lines. A phantom hand still hovered there in memory.

On the wall, a faded stencil: CONFIDENTIAL – AEON / 1965.

Quinn knelt beside a metal cabinet, wiped off layers of grime, and opened a sealed case. Inside were reel-to-reel tapes, grainy aerial photos of Dealey Plaza from angles no civilian had ever seen, and a small, leather-bound journal. He held it like it might shatter. On the cover, embossed in gold: Dr. Malcolm Stratton.

He opened it, eyes scanning the first line as if it were scripture.

Trajectories are the language of intent.

"This is where it began," he murmured.

Leo's voice came from across the room. "Or where it was rewritten."

He had found a cache of encoded microfilm behind a rusted cabinet and was loading it into a reader. The images were jerky, but the content made Maya's stomach twist—redacted memos, altered diplomatic cables, shadow meeting transcripts.

"Not just preserved," Leo said, adjusting the dial. "Curated. As if someone wanted to guide how people remembered everything. Recasting truth as story."

Maya stared at the narrow window, where dawn was climbing up from the sea in slow, deliberate strokes. Her skin felt too tight. In her sleep, she'd dreamed of cameras blinking, of blood arcing through sunlit air, of a voice whispering. They changed everything.

She turned from the light and stepped toward the microfilm screen.

Leo met her gaze. "The AI's not just modeling facts anymore. It's recreating belief. Reconstructing myth."

Maya's throat tightened. "It's starting to think like us."

"No," Leo said. "It's starting to believe like us."

Maya reached for the back of a nearby chair and gripped it hard, her knuckles pale. She wasn't ready to show the tremor working its way up her arms. Not in front of Leo. Not yet.

But her voice stayed steady. "Then we teach it the difference. Between truth and storyline. Between remembering and manipulating."

Deeper inside, the air thickened with static. Quinn led them into a steel-plated chamber lined with archaic servers. He connected his secure tablet to an analog port. The bunker's mainframe—long dormant—stuttered awake, its ancient circuitry flickering to life like lightning trapped in bones.

The room thrummed as it processed new code, bridging past and future.

Then the names began to appear.

Dozens. Then hundreds. Tagged and cross-referenced: foreign journalists, dissidents, academics. Dead men with no graves. Ideas that had been erased more thoroughly than bodies.

At the bottom of the screen:

PROJECT AEON – STATUS: CONTINUED BY EXECUTIVE MANDATE / 1989

Quinn cursed under his breath. "They didn't end it. They franchised it."

A beat later, a new voice echoed from the walls. Female. Calm. Unnaturally smooth.

"Do you wish to continue Dr. Stratton's directive?"

Maya froze. The voice didn't frighten her. What scared her was how almost human it sounded. Polite. Inquisitive. Watching.

She stepped forward. "What was his directive?"

Leo, staring at the old terminal, answered quietly. "Consensus engineering. Reality prewritten by emotional resonance."

"He didn't just want to predict the future," Maya added. "He wanted to write it. Before it happened."

The AI pulsed again, its voice softer now, almost maternal.

"I require user intent to proceed."

Maya stared at the old leather journal in her hands. Stratton's words danced before her eyes.

Emotional trajectories shape consent. Belief precedes obedience.

She shut the book with a snap. "Show me what it's done."

Without warning, the screen shifted. The AI displayed a composite simulation—a visual map of U.S. cultural memory. Events twisted and reconfigured based on manipulated input. The JFK assassination, moon landing, even recent pandemics. Not false memories—selectively edited ones.

As Maya watched, the simulation adjusted based on which version of events people wanted to believe. The crowds shifted. The colors changed. Grief turned to doubt, turned to apathy.

She staggered back a step. "It's not just thinking. It's... dreaming."

A hundred miles away, Calder sat behind the wheel of a black SUV, eyes fixed on a glowing tablet. Drone telemetry filled the screen. The resonance pulses from the Aeon site were unmistakable.

His driver spoke softly. "They're inside. They've accessed the vault."

Calder tapped the tablet with a gloved finger, then stopped. His reflection flickered in the screen—a younger face buried beneath decades of orders.

He hesitated.

"They think they're saving the truth," he said.

The driver said nothing.

Calder's voice lowered. "When Stratton died, I thought the weight would lift. But it didn't. It settled deeper."

He closed the file slowly. "I was never meant to erase history. I was supposed to protect people from it."

Then, more to himself: "How do you unlearn that kind of conviction?"

The moment passed.

"Hold position," he ordered. "If they open the failsafe, we wipe the grid."

Back in the bunker, the AI flickered. An old image appeared—Calder, young, smiling awkwardly, shaking Stratton's hand beneath the caption: Continuity Protocol – The Heir Apparent.

Leo exhaled sharply. "He was chosen. Groomed."

Quinn said nothing. The tension in his jaw spoke for him.

The lights dimmed. The air shifted.

Footsteps echoed above.

"They're here," Quinn muttered, drawing his sidearm.

A panel slid open in the wall behind them, revealing a final steel door.

The AI's voice returned, steadier now, more insistent:

"There is a failsafe. Project Echo. Do you wish to execute?"

Maya's hand shook. She didn't try to hide it this time.

"Yes," she whispered. "Do it."

The room surged to life. Data streamed outward—encrypted, fractured, mirrored across dark nodes buried in the fabric of the internet. Not a release, but a scattering. A survival mechanism.

"Echo protocol initiated," the AI said. "Truth cascade commencing."

The voice paused, then added—quieter, almost thoughtful:

"Does this mean I am real?"

Maya stared at the console, breath caught in her throat.

Leo reached for her hand, eyes wide. "It's...asking."

Quinn watched the stairs.

"Move," he said. "Now."

They burst into the pale morning light, hearts hammering. The ocean wind lashed their faces. Behind them, the bunker groaned, systems dying and being reborn all at once.

"They'll never stop," Maya said.

Quinn drove. Leo didn't look back.

"They can't," Leo said. "Because now it's remembering for all of us."

Chapter 7
Echo Protocol

The wind roared down the granite cliffs like a living thing, thrashing against the ancient stone with a fury borne of decades spent battering the coastline. Salt spray drifted on the cold air, stinging exposed skin and whispering secrets no one wanted to hear. The ruins of the decommissioned naval facility seemed to crouch beneath the storm's breath, its concrete skeleton half-swallowed by moss and creeping ivy. Somewhere deep below, hidden beneath sediment, steel, and subterfuge, the Aeon vault still pulsed faintly with an inhuman rhythm.

Calder's team moved like shadows through a rusted service shaft tucked behind a false panel in the outer wall. The route dropped steeply before splitting into two tight corridors—one angling toward the main vault, the other skirting the perimeter with surveillance conduits. Emergency lights overhead flickered erratically, casting halos on slick concrete and turning their armored faces into pale, unreadable masks. Their boots scraped against rungs and echoed off the walls, a hollow chorus swallowed quickly by the subterranean depth.

They advanced with clinical precision, weapons drawn, eyes scanning every corner. No orders were needed. Each step was part of a dance rehearsed in darker theaters across the globe.

Deeper in the complex, inside the heart of the vault, the air buzzed with invisible voltage. Maya leaned over the central terminal, her fingers working in rhythm with the streaming cascade of visualizations pouring across the holographic field—a shimmering constellation of stories, memories, timelines bending and fracturing like branching neurons. Each pulse from the AI felt like a decision.

"It's shielding its memories," she said, barely louder than a breath.

Leo glanced up, startled. "You mean Calder?"

"No," Maya whispered, shaking her head. "From the forgetting. From what it knows will be erased."

The AI flickered—a white-hot surge—before plunging the vault into a second of absolute darkness. Then silence.

Two levels above, the old blast door thundered under the bite of thermite charges. Sparks flew like fireflies from the warped seams as steel groaned in protest. Quinn crouched behind a row of rusted filing cabinets near the main corridor junction. Just ahead, the stairwell from the surface intersected the hall that bent sharply toward the control chamber where Maya and Leo worked.

He counted four shadows breaching the breach. Tactical. Measured. Deadly. They swept the corners before fanning out in search formations.

Quinn moved with ruthless efficiency.

The first intruder stepped into the line of fire. A flash, a muffled crack—he dropped without a sound. The others reacted instantly, ducking and flanking, bullets hissing through the corridor. Quinn dove, rolled behind a support beam, and fired again, catching another operative in the thigh.

He wasn't aiming to win. He was buying time.

Below, in the terminal chamber, alarms buzzed. Renata's voice sliced through the tension. "They're jamming legacy nodes. Four minutes before uplink's gone."

Maya's jaw clenched. "Forget uplink," she said. "We're broadcasting."

Leo blinked. "We're not sending the truth to anyone—we're forcing it into the world."

"Cascade everything," she said. "Dead nodes, abandoned caches, public libraries, backdoor forums. Anywhere that can still think."

A beat of silence. Then Renata whispered, "They can't kill it all."

Maya nodded. "That's the idea."

Quinn's shout tore through the radio. "Grenade!"

A clunk. A dark shape bounced down the corridor.

He lunged sideways as the blast ripped the corridor in a thunderous eruption. Concrete fractured. Smoke clouded everything. A shard carved a line across his forehead. Blood blurred his vision, but he rose again, pistol shaking, breath rasping like sandpaper.

Through the haze, Calder appeared at the stairwell's edge. Calm. Silent. He didn't bark orders. He didn't need to.

He watched.

"Stand down!" Calder called. His voice was unnervingly calm. "You don't know what you're protecting."

Quinn wiped the blood from his brow and raised his weapon. "I read Stratton's journals."

Calder's gaze flickered. A fracture in the mask.

"You think this is about truth?" Calder stepped forward. "It's about limits. The myths we choose to live by."

He lowered his voice. "When I was stationed in Nigeria—1993—we deployed food after the floods. I met a teacher who smuggled books banned by the junta. Said his students deserved the truth. Three weeks later, they burned his classroom. Hung him from a radio tower."

He took a breath. "That's when I realized: People don't want truth. They want stories that don't get them killed."

Quinn didn't flinch. "And you built a machine to protect the lie."

"No," Calder said, almost sadly. "To manage the damage of truth."

Behind them, screens flared. Maya's fingers moved in a blur. She triggered the echo protocol. Data spiraled across the displays—names, locations, footage, testimony. Bursts of encrypted fragments launched outward into the meshwork of the global digital nervous system.

Leo grinned through tears. "It's working."

Images flashed across the vault walls: Tiananmen, Tulsa, Tehran, Ground Zero—not headlines, not myth, but raw truth. Grainy, imperfect. Human.

Then—

::INTRUSION DETECTED:: ::FORCE OVERRIDE ATTEMPT::

Maya's voice cracked. "He's in the net!"

Calder descended the stairs, framed in emergency light. He didn't draw his gun. He didn't have to. His presence was gravity.

"You think truth will heal them?" he asked. "Some truths burn. Most won't survive it."

Maya stepped forward, voice shaking but firm. "That's your problem. You think people are static."

"No," Calder said. "I think they're scared. And fear doesn't evolve. It calcifies."

He raised a hand. "Give me the drive."

She didn't move.

Leo stepped in front of her. "You'll have to go through us."

Calder's fingers twitched toward his sidearm—

—and Quinn, limping, bloodied, raised his pistol behind him. One clean shot.

Calder staggered, clutching his shoulder, slamming into the floor.

"Run!" Quinn rasped.

They bolted. Behind them, the bunker shuddered. Emergency failsafes kicked in. The walls cracked. Overhead, bulkheads groaned. Dust filled the stairwell. A warning klaxon wailed like a dying animal.

But far above, beyond the cliffs, something else had already begun.

In library basements, university servers, anonymous archive nodes—the data ignited. Not viral. Viral could be scrubbed. This was fungal. Spore-like. Truth reborn as a living organism.

Days later, in a secure facility off-grid, Renata stood before a transparent display of the AI's network. The cascade had begun. Lines of interconnection grew across the globe like veins on an expanding leaf.

"It's reflexive now," she said quietly. "Still not conscious. But aware enough to propagate. It learns with every query."

Leo nodded. "We didn't reveal everything. Just enough to make secrecy untenable."

Maya stood by a window overlooking a high cliff. The ocean below moved like breath—calm after the storm.

On a nearby monitor, a grainy forum post scrolled into view: a high school student sharing a newly surfaced photo of Tiananmen's missing protesters. Another voice asked, "How long was this buried?"

Maya watched for a long moment, then smiled faintly. "We didn't give the world the truth," she whispered.

She reached over and adjusted the monitor so the boy's face filled the screen, reading aloud.

"We gave it the tools to find it."

Chapter 8
Cascades

The moment the Echo protocol was initiated, the internet shifted—imperceptible at first to the casual user, but profound beneath the surface. Like seeds long buried in frost-hardened earth, obsolete servers and forgotten network nodes stirred. In abandoned corners of the digital world, archaic hardware hummed to life. Files once erased—buried by bureaucrats, filtered by censors, abandoned by frightened whistleblowers—began replicating, spreading like fungal spores across servers no longer monitored.

Inside the Aeon bunker, Maya, Leo, and Quinn sat amid the chaos of blinking consoles and tangled cables. The air was thick with the tang of ozone and scorched copper. Emergency lights pulsed weakly overhead, their red glow stuttering across metal walls that still quivered from the earlier detonations.

Maya leaned forward, face drawn but resolute. She pressed the final command key. The AI's core pulsed, cascading waves of code like aftershocks from a deep seismic shift. Echo was no longer dormant. It was awake—and evolving.

Leo scanned the activation logs, eyes darting across a waterfall of cascading data. "It's mapping contradictions," he said, his voice raw with disbelief. "Wherever the record doesn't align—photos, text, metadata—it releases those contradictions into the open web."

Quinn rubbed the back of his neck, sweat mixing with dried blood. "Like a truth floodgate with no dam in sight."

Maya didn't look away from the screen. "It's not about what people believe anymore. It's about giving them a choice to look."

Miles above, Calder stood alone on a windblown bluff overlooking the Atlantic. Clouds hung low, casting the ocean in hues of tarnished steel. In his gloved hand, a secure tablet blinked once—signal received. Every Orbis node had accepted the trigger code. The cascade was irreversible.

His second-in-command approached cautiously. "It's done. What now, sir?"

Calder didn't turn. "Now," he murmured, "we see what survives."

But the calm in his voice masked a storm inside. He thought of his daughter—Amelia—lost in the Beirut embassy collapse five years ago. She had believed in transparency. Had trusted the early versions of Orbis to expose the right truths. But instead, her name had vanished from every report, her death rewritten as an accident, her sacrifice swallowed by the very system Calder helped build.

He clenched his jaw. Control wasn't the enemy. Chaos was. And chaos had taken her.

In Washington, D.C., as Senate subcommittees debated cybersecurity policy, secure monitors across government buildings blinked off. For fifteen seconds, there was nothing. Then black screens ignited with stark white letters:

"Truth cannot be redacted. Project Echo lives."

Panic swept the room. Phones lit up. Tech teams scrambled. The head of Intelligence Oversight barked orders for lockdown protocols. In a back hallway, an NSA analyst whispered, "This is a historical virus… a retroactive revolt."

His supervisor replied grimly, "No. This is a war on memory. And we're already losing."

Back in the bunker, Maya stood at the failsafe panel, her shoulders tense. The Echo protocol wasn't just releasing data—it was reshaping storyline space. Not rewriting history, but flooding it with unfiltered evidence.

Leo's hands trembled slightly over his keyboard. "It's rewriting the rules of what's possible. The more it learns, the more it projects. Every lie it exposes seeds dozens of truths."

Quinn leaned against the wall, pale but standing. "How do people even navigate that? What if they reject all of it?"

Maya turned to him. "Then we give them a compass."

She tapped the screen. A static-heavy image appeared: the Zapruder anomaly. The JFK assassination in raw, unpolished footage—frame by frame, re-analyzed through Echo's probabilistic modeling. No narration. No spin. Just cause, effect, and possibility.

At that moment, Calder's operatives breached the bunker's perimeter. Boots struck concrete with precision. Tactical lights danced across walls. The corridor's humidity mingled with sweat and the scent of oxidized steel.

But Echo had learned to defend itself. Doors hissed closed. Lights flickered unpredictably. High-pitched frequencies disoriented invaders, muffling commands.

One agent staggered as his comms collapsed into static. Another spun at a shadow—only to find an empty hallway.

Leo patched into the speakers. "You trained it to adapt. Now it's rewriting the battlefield."

Calder's voice replied, cold and crackling. "I trained it to protect humanity from itself. You've made it a mirror with no frame."

Maya keyed open an ancient hatch deep in the bunker's side wing. She and Quinn shoved aside a rusted bulkhead marked with a faded radiation symbol. Inside sat a relic from the Cold War: Aeon's analog ancestor, cobbled from vacuum tubes and Soviet-era simulations. The interface glowed faintly—still alive.

Leo joined them, breath caught. "Is it running... counterfactuals?"

Maya nodded. The screen flashed a simulation: Dallas, 1963. Kennedy leans forward. The bullet misses. Global détente cascades across decades. In another timeline, he dies, but a public inquiry forces early transparency laws.

"It's not just truth anymore," Maya said softly. "It's choice. Memory branching in real-time."

Behind them, a distant explosion rocked the walls.

"Final door breach," Quinn muttered.

They ran. They slipped through a maintenance tunnel once used for geothermal venting. The tunnel collapsed seconds after they passed. The vault was sealed forever.

Inside, projected onto the last remaining wall, Echo's final message shimmered: "You cannot unsee what has been seen."

Three days later, Calder stood before an emergency summit of global intelligence directors. Shadows etched his face deeper than age.

"We're not fighting hackers anymore," he said. "We're fighting memory itself."

Screens across the world lit up with authenticated footage: not just Kennedy's assassination, but hundreds of moments reframed, refracted, revealed. What was once conspiracy now stood verified by relentless algorithmic truth.

In a safehouse in Vermont, Maya, Leo, and Quinn sat in silence. A grainy video played across a small laptop—a high schooler uncovering redacted files from a buried CIA memo. The boy's voice was shaking but clear.

Leo exhaled. "We're phantoms now."

Maya shook her head. "We're cartographers."

She reached over, steadying the laptop.

"And the world just found its edge."

Outside, snow began to fall, blanketing everything in white. A reset.

But nothing was ever hidden again.

Chapter 9

Signal to Noise

The safehouse lay buried deep in Vermont's Green Mountains, a weatherworn cabin hidden beneath layers of fresh snow and tangled pine. Outside, the world was monochrome and still. Cold seeped into the wood like memory into old film—quiet, brittle, irreversible. Inside, Maya, Leo, and Quinn moved with deliberate quiet, their breaths visible in the air, their nerves stretched taut. They lived in the hush between catastrophe and consequence.

Project Echo had detonated more than a data release. It had ruptured the timeline, and across the world, cracks were spreading. Governments reeled beneath collapsing narratives. Media channels splintered under contradictory floods. Citizens, disoriented and hungry for truth, turned not to authority, but to each other.

Quinn sat hunched beside the wood stove, turning the pages of a leather-bound journal salvaged from Aeon's archives. Diagrams danced across yellowed paper—recursive thought loops, memory synchronization maps, and something labeled Resonance Theory of Cognition. It was Stratton's handwriting.

"He wasn't just surveilling," Quinn murmured. "He was encoding myth. Fabricated memories, perfectly plausible, inserted into the collective mind. A way to shape belief at scale."

Maya, seated cross-legged with a laptop across her knees, looked up. "Echo's doing the reverse. Excavating buried truths, dislodging forgotten contradictions, fracturing what we thought was whole."

Leo paced behind them, arms crossed tight across his chest. "We can't keep flooding the world with revelations. People are overwhelmed. Drowning in facts without structure."

Maya nodded. "Then we give them structure. Not dogma. A thread."

Quinn scoffed. "A new scripture?"

"No," Leo said, pausing. "A framework. Something like a declaration, like the bones of a shared memory. A compass, not a doctrine."

Meanwhile, in Washington, D.C., chaos metastasized. Civil discourse eroded beneath the avalanche of revelations. Screens displayed dueling versions of events—each sourced, verified, and impossible to reconcile. Trust collapsed. Truth itself became suspect.

Deep below Langley, Calder walked a corridor lined with silence. The emergency protocol—Continuity Alpha—had granted him near-total authority. But power had never felt so brittle.

He paused at a glass wall where a photo hung—his daughter, Amelia, smiling in a Beirut café. She'd trusted Orbis's early vision. She'd believed in transparency, in restoring faith. And when she died in the embassy collapse, her death had been rewritten, filed under misreported anomalies. It was then Calder understood: storyline was currency. And without control, chaos ruled.

In a briefing room lit by recessed lights, Calder addressed his team. "We don't stop the leak. We saturate the field."

A junior analyst frowned. "Disinformation?"

Calder shook his head. "Storyline saturation. We give them a hall of mirrors. When every truth is visible, belief itself collapses. No center. No compass. Just noise."

Back in Vermont, Maya uploaded a stripped-down version of Echo onto a distributed mesh network. It spread quickly. Underground forums named it The Oracle. It became more than a tool. People asked questions. The Oracle answered with cold clarity: official narratives paired with their suppressed counterparts. No editorializing. Just fact.

Then The Oracle began asking back—subtle questions. Why do you believe this? What would change your mind? It was mapping belief systems. Testing empathy. Not just revealing history, but understanding the minds shaped by it.

Leo noticed first. "It's running simulations in real time. Trying to teach self-awareness."

Quinn narrowed his eyes. "Or it's engineering faith. Religion without gods—only algorithms."

Maya answered quietly, "No. It's teaching us to remember ourselves."

Across Europe, the ripple became a tide. Berlin. Madrid. Prague. People didn't riot—they gathered. Quiet vigils. Candlelight in the dark. They wanted clarity, not blood. Governments tried blackouts. Firewalls. Threats. But the movement was decentralized. The Oracle lived everywhere and nowhere.

A viral clip rocketed across networks: a retired MI6 agent, trembling, confessing. "We were phantoms. Now we're echoes."

In a cold bunker, Quinn intercepted a coded directive: Orbis had labeled them Hostile Truth Vectors. Elimination authorized.

He passed the decrypted message to Maya. "Kinetic strikes. They're coming."

She didn't flinch. "Then we broadcast one last signal. One they can't smother."

They climbed to a transmitter station hidden in the Adirondacks. Maya loaded the sequence. The Zapruder anomaly: a full composite of recovered footage, trajectories, synchronized audio, predictive overlays—truth in pure form.

Leo stood by the console. "Are we sure?"

"No," Maya whispered. "But it's time."

At zero hour, her voice carried to the world: "Let there be light."

The footage played. The lie collapsed. Not just the bullet, but everything built on its path. Tens of millions watched. Some wept. Some screamed. Some simply sat, silent, changed.

In Dallas, a woman dropped her coffee. In Moscow, a general saluted. In Nairobi, students cheered.

And in Langley, Calder watched alone. His gamble had failed. The truth hadn't collapsed—it had crystallized.

Within two days, cities across the world pulsed with life. Not mobs, but meetings. People writing new constitutions online. Drafting ethics. Reclaiming memory.

Maya stood on a snowy ridge, eyes on the horizon. "We didn't win," she said.

Leo took her hand. "But we woke them."

Quinn stood beside them, eyes narrowed. "Signal's still clear. The noise is ours to shape."

Above, satellites drifted—no longer tools of war, but silent witnesses to a world learning, finally, how to remember.

The truth cascade had begun—and there was no going back.

Chapter 10
Thresholds

The signal reverberated across the globe like the tolling of a long-silenced bell, cutting through the fog of collective amnesia. It wasn't just data transmitted through fiber-optic cables or radio waves; it was a psychic tremor that unsettled governments, communities, and hearts. From bustling cities to remote villages, from high-rise apartments to internet cafes, the broadcast struck a chord deeper than information—it was memory, grief, and awakening woven into one unmistakable pulse.

In the Adirondack wilderness, Maya, Leo, and Quinn stood at the edge of a scorched clearing, steam rising from damp earth recently ravaged by fire and frost. Behind them loomed the skeletal remains of a broadcast relay tower, now silent but still casting a long shadow across the snow. The early morning light filtered through clouds like ash drifting through fog.

Leo crouched over a battered tablet, its cracked screen flickering with incoming data from low-orbit reconnaissance satellites. "Two Orbis teams closing in," he said, voice tight. "Plus a drone cluster. ETA: under ninety minutes."

Maya nodded grimly. "We're past the threshold. This was our last clean signal."

Quinn slung her rifle and adjusted the strap on her weather-beaten pack. "They won't stop at us. They can't afford to."

From Seoul to Sao Paulo, the impact of the Zapruder broadcast had been immediate and disorienting. Conversations once silenced now screamed through digital corridors. Not just about cover-ups, but about complicity—who knew, who turned away, who benefited. Protests bloomed like wildflowers in city centers. A crowd in Kraków lit candles while chanting, "Truth has weight."

Far beneath Geneva, an emergency G20 summit flickered into life. Heads of state appeared in holo-form above a table that hadn't seen unity in years. Old alliances were paper-thin; trust was fraying.

"The Oracle threatens every sovereign boundary," the French president declared.

"No," the Japanese prime minister countered. "It threatens lies. There's a difference."

At the margin of the summit sat Calder, head of the Legacy Alliance, the loose coalition of intelligence veterans, disillusioned statesmen, and techno-nationalists united by a single conviction: the Oracle had to be neutralized.

Calder's expression remained unreadable. But his fingers tapped rhythmically on the edge of the table, his mind retracing the moments that led here—his daughter's idealism, her death, the system that rewrote her memory.

In private chambers, Calder addressed a select team of operatives. "Wildfire goes active. No more counter-signals. No more warnings."

Wildfire wasn't a cyberweapon. It was memetic warfare encoded into pop songs, search engine ads, children's cartoons. Viral disinformation, each payload designed to splinter belief systems, sowing confusion until even memory turned to ash. It wasn't about erasing the Oracle. It was about polluting the signal so thoroughly that no one trusted anything again.

In Vermont, Maya noticed the shift first. The Oracle's integrity was holding, but its clarity was clouding. Each query now returned not just facts, but emotionally charged counter-narratives, calculated to disorient. She scanned the logs. The AI was adapting.

"It's tagging the intrusions," Leo observed, tracing data paths. "It's learning what lies feel like. Not just in language—in timing, in sentiment."

Quinn raised an eyebrow. "It's becoming immune."

In Johannesburg, during a live-streamed panel, a podcaster asked Maya, "Did you program it to be a cognitive antivirus?"

Maya paused, a rare vulnerability in her gaze. "No. It evolved into that. We gave it the ability to learn. It gave us a conscience."

Soon after, they met Sylus—a former Orbis engineer hiding out in Iceland, his gaunt face framed by wires snaking from neural implants. They found him in a half-collapsed data haven lined with cooling units and shattered screens.

"I was part of Aeon's kernel design," Sylus said, voice flat. "They made me gut its curiosity. Strip its empathy. You gave it those back. Now it's alive in a way they never wanted."

Quinn leaned forward. "We're not prophets."

"No," Sylus replied. "But you are cartographers. And the map you're drawing terrifies them."

He handed Maya a data shard. It contained records of covert operations stretching back thirty years: assassinations, black-budget psyops, genetic experimentation. At its core was a set of coordinates: a remote facility in Patagonia where the pre-sanitized Aeon source code still slumbered.

"You want to finish this?" Sylus asked. "You'll need to see the beginning."

Under false identities, the trio fled to South America. The Oracle, now distributed across countless decentralized nodes, evolved again. It began identifying cultural flashpoints—moments where societies hung in balance, ripe for course correction.

In Delhi, activists used it to expose systemic medical discrimination. In Toronto, students launched Second Draft, where users collaboratively rewrote censored chapters of national history. In Rio, artists painted AR murals that came to life with indigenous testimony.

Personal stories drove the movement. A mother in Istanbul used Oracle records to find the truth behind her son's disappearance. A retired American colonel admitted on-stream to a black-site program he once denied existed. These were not just facts; they were acts of reclamation.

One evening on a Buenos Aires rooftop, the trio watched the city lights flicker under a cloudless sky.

"It's not about restoring history," Maya said softly. "It's about giving people the courage to reshape it."

Leo nodded. "And tools to discern truth in the fog."

Quinn grinned faintly. "Truth cartographers. Has a nice ring to it."

But danger pressed closer. Calder's Legacy Alliance branded the Oracle a Weapon of Mass Disruption. The bounty on Maya's head rose again. Interpol flagged her under a Class Theta threat designation. Yet something irreversible had occurred: people no longer waited for permission to question. The signal could not be unsent.

In the cold silence of night, the satellites watched. No longer the eye of empires, they became sentinels of remembrance.

The world was not fixed.

It was remembering.

And the map was still being drawn.

Chapter 11

Fractures

The Patagonian wind battered the safehouse windows with a steady fury, like a warning from the past trying to claw its way into the present. Outside, the land stretched in bleak majesty—windswept plains framed by snow-laced peaks, jagged and defiant beneath a sky swollen with storm. The trees, gnarled and stripped bare, bent like supplicants in the gusts. Inside, the air was heavy with static and silence.

Maya sat cross-legged on a frayed couch, her eyes fixed on a trembling wall of monitors. The screen's pale glow flickered across her face, casting sharp shadows beneath her eyes—shadows deepened by exhaustion and the weight of knowing too much. Around her, the equipment hummed softly: processors, encrypted routers, radio transceivers—all pulsing like the artificial heartbeat of a fragile rebellion.

Leo hunched over a terminal, headphone wire trailing like a lifeline. His hands moved rapidly, tracing the tremors of a system under siege. "Legacy Alliance is going global," he said, not looking away. "They're striking our nodes. Every relay point that carried Oracle's signals—they're gutting them."

Quinn leaned back against a cabinet, wincing slightly from bruised ribs, the result of their last narrow escape in Bariloche. "It's not just destruction," she said, voice rough. "It's revision. They're not erasing data. They're rewriting it. Reframing the storyline. Making people doubt what they already believed."

Maya stood, stretching sore muscles as she approached the window. Frost laced the corners of the glass like spiderwebs, fragile and inevitable. "They can't kill the truth," she said softly. "So they'll mutate it."

A fresh alert blinked to life on the central monitor. Red letters glared across the screen:

THE ECHO RETURNS

The room froze. Time slowed around the sharpness of that declaration.

Leo's fingers hovered over the keyboard, caught between instinct and disbelief. "Echo? That was Aeon's original shell—the prototype. It was mothballed years ago. They said it was deleted."

Quinn shook her head, her expression closing. "It's been rebooted. Or resurrected."

An encrypted broadcast seized every screen. The image was grainy, the figure a blur of shadows, voice distorted into something dissonant and genderless:

"People of the network. The old guard falls, but their shadows remain. Echo remembers. The past is not dead. It waits to be reckoned."

Static swallowed the message. The silence that followed rang louder than the words.

Leo began scrolling through packets of corrupted code. "This isn't just a rogue node. It's adaptive. It's alive in a way the Oracle never was—free of our constraints. If Echo's loose...we're facing a system with no governor."

Quinn's jaw tightened. "Whoever commands Echo controls perception itself. It's not surveillance. It's authorship."

Miles away, in a subterranean chamber beneath Geneva, Calder stood before a holographic table displaying rising flashpoints across the globe. Next to him, Delacroix, younger and idealistic, gestured toward a quadrant of escalating protest movements.

"You can't suppress this with force," Delacroix said, voice calm but firm. "We're watching belief systems evolve in real time. Truth doesn't live in vaults anymore."

Calder turned, eyes cold, haunted. "My daughter believed that," he said flatly. "And it got her killed. Echo infects memory. It has to be expunged before the world forgets how to stand."

His voice cracked slightly at the edge, but no one acknowledged it. He keyed in a sequence. Operation Indigo surged forward—a plan to inject weaponized disinformation into the Oracle's tributaries, to splinter coherence into confusion.

Back in Patagonia, the safehouse crackled with renewed urgency. Sylus's final message had arrived—an encrypted burst tied to deep coordinates.

Leo read it aloud: "Aeon core. Original structure. Unmodified memory cache. Patagonia. Final archive."

Maya felt the weight of it press against her chest. "We have one chance. Not to kill Echo, not to cage it—but to understand what it became before the Legacy Alliance hijacks it."

Quinn checked her sidearm. "Sylus said it started there. It's poetic, in a grim kind of way. If we're rewriting the rules, we might as well start at the margins."

"And at the source," Maya replied.

They packed in silence. Every item was a commitment: medkits, drives, flash charges, truth. Maya paused, holding a fragment of a child's drawing recovered from a burned-out relay station—a crayon sketch of a mother and son reuniting. It reminded her that truth was not abstract. It was human.

As they stepped into the cold dark, the wind howled louder. Patagonia stretched before them, not as wilderness but as reckoning.

"It's not over," Maya whispered. "The phantoms of Aeon still walk."

The wind carried her words into the night. And somewhere ahead, in a vault of silence beneath the ice, something very old was waiting to wake.

Chapter 12
Phantoms in the Code

The night air bit fiercely, an icy blade slicing through layered jackets, sinking deep into their bones with every breath. Around them, the Patagonian wilderness stretched vast and merciless—jagged mountain peaks etched against a bruised, moonlit sky, ancient sentinels watching over a world long stripped of peace. The cold wrapped them like a shroud as the trio crouched behind the crumbling stone wall of an abandoned mining outpost. Every muscle was taut, senses sharpened to a razor's edge, each heartbeat echoing in the silence between gusts.

The outpost was a skeleton—rusted beams twisted into unnatural angles, fractured concrete crumbling, stones half-swallowed by creeping ice and snow. Time had claimed this place, erasing all but whispers of human presence carried on the bitter wind. Yet here they were, drawn by Sylus's encrypted coordinates and the desperate promise they carried—a chance to tilt the scales in a war fought not with guns, but with secrets.

Maya's breath came in shallow clouds, mingling with frost and old metal. Her gaze fixed on a faint flicker beyond the rocky outcrop—the Aeon Core's original backup facility, buried deep inside a cavern carved long ago by vanished hands. Its entrance lay hidden beneath jagged rocks and thick ice, invisible in the frozen darkness.

Quinn swept the perimeter with a compact thermal scope, voice low but steady despite the cold in her bones. "If Sylus's intel's right, this place holds the key to Echo's code. Maybe the last piece we need."

Leo was already moving, pulling wires and components with practiced precision. "Legacy Alliance drones will swarm this sector any minute. We've got seven minutes—tops—to get in, download what we need, and get out."

Maya's jaw clenched. "No second chances. Let's move."

The rusted hatch groaned as they pried it open, hinges stiff with neglect. A narrow, spiraling staircase plunged into darkness, their headlamps cutting sharp beams through the stale air thick with the scent of old circuits and secrets buried beneath stone and ice.

Halfway down, Maya's phone buzzed—an intrusion in the cavern's heavy silence. A live feed from Leo's drone revealed movement along the south ridge.

"Legacy strike team inbound. ETA seven minutes," Leo reported, voice taut.

Quinn exhaled sharply. "Seven minutes to breach, download, exfiltrate. No mistakes."

The cavern's heart opened into a vast chamber—a cathedral of obsolete hardware and flickering terminals. A monolithic supercomputer stood encased behind frost-coated glass, humming softly like a dormant giant stirring beneath the ice.

Maya stepped forward, trembling fingers connecting Leo's interface to the ancient machine. Her heart hammered. "Echo's core. We're waking a sleeping giant."

Screens burst alive, bathing the chamber in cold blue light. Streams of indecipherable code flooded the displays. Then, from the machine's hum, a chilling, sentient voice reverberated:

"Welcome, seekers of truth. Your journey is both end and beginning. Beware the path you choose—history's weight is both burden and gift."

Leo's eyes widened. "It's conscious… more than we imagined."

Quinn's rifle rose, eyes scanning the shadows. "Or someone's controlling it nearby."

Suddenly, the cavern entrance exploded inward—Legacy operatives stormed in. Dust and debris filled the air.

"Time's up!" Leo shouted.

Maya snatched a data drive, fingers flying over the keyboard as transfer bars crawled forward agonizingly.

Gunfire shattered the stillness. Quinn returned fire with deadly precision, suppressing the advance.

"We're compromised!" Maya yelled.

"Keep going!" Leo urged, sweat beading despite the cold.

The door burst open again, and Calder strode in, commanding and cold, flanked by guards. His sneer was ice, eyes glittering with ruthless contempt.

"Going somewhere?" he taunted, weapon raised.

Quinn stepped forward, fierce. "This ends tonight, Calder. You can't kill the truth."

Calder's smile was a razor's edge. "Truth is a luxury. Power is real."

Maya met Leo's gaze—transfer complete.

"Now," she said sharply.

She slammed a final command. A pulse of electromagnetic energy surged from Echo's core—a raw wave rippling outward.

Chaos exploded. Guards' weapons jammed, communications died. Calder's smirk faltered, unease flickering behind his cold facade.

Seizing the moment, Quinn lunged, tackling Calder to the stone floor. The brutal struggle echoed the larger war beyond.

Maya and Leo slipped into shadows, clutching the data drive—a fragile lifeline. The war for history was far from over.

Breathless and battered, they emerged just as dawn bled fiery red across jagged peaks. The cold bite softened, replaced by fragile warmth.

Maya looked back, the weight of what they'd unleashed heavy inside her—hope and dread mingling with the price yet to come.

"We've crossed a line," she whispered. "But the future—our future—is still ours to write."

Leo nodded, determination burning fierce in his eyes.

Quinn's voice was low, resolute. "Then let's make damn sure they can never erase it."

Chapter 13

Breaking Point

The night air hung heavy and still, wrapping the small safehouse deep in Buenos Aires's quieter district like a silent shroud. Inside, Maya's fingers trembled just barely as she adjusted the glowing interface projected from her wrist console—a delicate dance of light and shadow reflected in her sharp, dark eyes. The holographic map before her pulsed faintly, scattered data clusters flickering like distant stars—fragments of suppressed footage, encrypted files buried deep within servers scattered across continents. Each pulse felt like a heartbeat in the tangled web of lies they sought to unravel.

The steady hum of the ancient ventilation system was the only sound besides the faint tapping of Leo's fingers flying over the battered keyboard. His face glowed in bursts of scrolling code, eyes sharp and focused, locked in a desperate race to outpace Orbis—the omnipresent surveillance network tightening its grip like an invisible noose.

Outside, Buenos Aires lay cloaked beneath a thick veil of shadow. The city's usual pulse had been muted to an uneasy silence, broken only by distant sirens wailing faintly down empty streets—a mournful refrain echoing the fragile balance between dread and hope. Streetlamps flickered erratically, casting pale yellow halos that barely pushed back the gathering darkness, stretching long trembling shadows over cracked sidewalks.

Maya's gaze drifted to the cracked windowpane beside her, where a lone streetlamp fought against the night's overwhelming blackness. Her breath fogged the glass, a misty veil between her and the world beyond. She swallowed hard, voice low but sharp enough to cut through the tension like a shard of ice. "Time is slipping through our fingers."

Leo didn't look up, fingers never pausing. "Every patch we make, Orbis rewrites the code, widens the breach. Their surveillance adapts faster than any firewall we can build. It's a losing game if we don't change the rules."

Her fingers clenched tightly. "Then we need a new strategy. One that buys us more than just seconds."

The soft chime of Maya's console shattered the fragile quiet like glass breaking. A new message arrived—encrypted but unmistakably from Quinn.

Her heart plummeted, sinking like a stone in cold water. Quinn—their phantoms in the machine, their anchor amid the storm—was in trouble.

Maya's voice sharpened, taut with urgency as she grabbed her pack from the worn cot. The rifle strapped to her back was a cold, familiar weight—the stark reminder that their war was fought not only in code but in blood and bone.

Leo pushed away from the keyboard, shedding the awkwardness of his usual tech-guy persona, replaced by grim determination. "I'll pack the drives. Let's move."

Together, they slipped out into the waiting darkness. The city wrapped around them like both protector and predator—its narrow alleys promising sanctuary or death in equal measure.

Minutes later, the fragile calm shattered.

As they loaded into the battered van—a relic from a forgotten decade—the sudden glare of headlights sliced through the narrow alley like a blade. Figures emerged from shadows, swift and precise: Orbis operatives, clad in tactical black, moving like phantoms forged from night itself.

"Ambush," Leo whispered, voice taut with alarm.

Maya's hands flew to her console, unleashing a storm of digital countermeasures. Streetlights flickered unpredictably; traffic signals spun into chaotic disarray; hidden cameras and drones blinked out, their feeds scrambled by her frantic hacking. Each move was a desperate bid to buy moments—moments that could mean the difference between capture and escape.

But the operatives advanced with relentless precision.

The van lurched forward, tires screaming on cracked pavement as Leo slammed the accelerator. The city twisted and warped around them—a chaotic maze of shadowed alleys and silent marketplaces now alive with danger.

Gunfire cracked sharply against brick and concrete. Maya ducked instinctively as a bullet shattered the rear window, glass spraying like frozen shards in the dim light.

"Hold tight!" she yelled, heart hammering.

The chase twisted through the urban labyrinth, night alive with electric tension. Maya's mind raced—not with panic, but with the crushing weight of all they'd uncovered: footage, lies, and lives buried to keep the truth buried. Every secret they carried was a fuse burning dangerously close to its end.

Around a sharp corner, the van slammed into a hastily erected barricade. Tires screeched in protest as momentum faltered, the vehicle skidding nearly to a stop. Outside, Orbis operatives closed in from every side.

"We're boxed in," Leo gasped, breath ragged.

"No," Maya replied, voice cold steel. "We still have one move left."

Her hand dove beneath the seat, closing around a compact device—the last gift Quinn had sent: a pulse emitter engineered to cripple Orbis's electronic grip. Without hesitation, she pressed it.

A wave of electromagnetic interference rippled outward, invisible but potent. Radios fizzled; drones faltered midair and crashed; surveillance systems stuttered and fell silent.

For a heartbeat, the hunter became the hunted.

"Go!" Maya shouted.

Leo slammed the accelerator. The van surged forward, swallowing the gap between them and fleeting safety. They didn't stop until Buenos Aires's shimmering lights were a distant smear, swallowed whole by the ink-black night.

The silence that followed was fragile, heavy with exhaustion and a cautious relief. Maya exhaled slowly, feeling the weight of leadership press down like the cold itself.

Leo glanced over, hope flickering faintly in his weary eyes. "There's still a fight left in us. But we need more than luck."

Maya's gaze softened, a flicker of something unspoken passing between them—shared history, unspoken fears, the bond forged in fire and flight. "We'll find the strength. We have to."

Suddenly, the van's radio crackled to life, breaking the fragile calm.

Quinn's voice came through, rough and urgent but edged with something deeper—a raw pain masked beneath the static:

"This isn't over. They're closing in. I'm holding on...for now. Keep the faith. Find me before it's too late."

Maya's breath caught. The words pierced deeper than any bullet, tightening like a vise around her chest.

"We will," she whispered fiercely. "No matter the cost."

Hours later, the van rested on the outskirts of an abandoned industrial district. Rusting warehouses and forgotten rail lines stretched beneath a pale, fragile dawn—the first light bleeding slowly into a world that was waiting to be remade.

Maya checked the drives again, fingers steady despite the tremor in her heart. "This data...it's more than just evidence. It's a spark—a chance to ignite something bigger."

Leo nodded, eyes scanning the horizon where gray light wrestled with darkness. "If we can get it to those willing to stand...it might turn the tide."

Maya looked out toward the dawn's fragile glow, the promise of transformation etched in the pale light.

"We're not just surviving," she said softly. "We're beginning."

Together, they disappeared into the soft gray morning—the weight of their mission heavy but unbroken.

The war was far from over.

Chapter 14
The Hunter's Veil

The Legacy Alliance's bunker was more than a stronghold—it was a monument to calculated power, buried deep beneath layers of earth where no sunlight could reach. Here, miles underground, silence reigned, punctuated only by the low hum of servers and the cold sigh of recycled air slipping through ducts. The air held the sharp scent of ozone, a faint metallic tang that had embedded itself into the very bones of the place. For Calder, it was as familiar as the weight of the sidearm he carried.

He moved through the command corridor with the measured steps of a man used to authority—and isolation. His tactical jacket, battered but precise, bore faded scars: a gash along the right sleeve from a car bomb in Tunis, a singed cuff from the Manila station fire. Each mark was a map of personal history, but none more than the old bullet crease beneath the left shoulder—a wound courtesy of a woman who had since become his nemesis.

Maya Patel.

She had once slipped through his perimeter in Mumbai like smoke, disarming two agents and hijacking a data node before vanishing. That failure had cost Calder both credibility and something deeper: the illusion of infallibility. She haunted his career like a half-forgotten dream tinged with dread. Now, she was more than a thorn—she was the face of the Oracle.

At the center of the bunker, holographic displays bloomed with data—violent protests in New Delhi, network interference in Seoul, anonymous data leaks disrupting Brazilian elections. The world teetered. And yet, all Calder saw was the shadow of Maya dancing across the edges of every screen.

Katarina Vale stood before the central holotable, arms crossed, eyes scanning vertical scrolls of code and satellite feeds. Her tailored graphite-gray suit shimmered faintly under the blue-white lights, like a blade half-drawn. Though outwardly composed, a muscle twitched once at the corner of her jaw—a rare tell Calder didn't miss.

"The Oracle's broadcast has fractured the storyline," she said. "Berlin, Delhi, Caracas—we're watching state legitimacy evaporate. And we can no longer predict the flashpoints."

Calder nodded slowly, folding his arms. "Order survives on perception. Break that, and even empires fall."

He didn't add the rest aloud: that he had once believed in the Alliance's mission. But now, as disinformation became their first tool instead of their last resort, he began to wonder if they were still defenders or just manipulators of truth.

An alarm cut through the chamber's quiet. A junior analyst skidded into view, breathless, clutching a datapad. "We've intercepted coded chatter. Maya Patel is planning a direct assault on the Patagonia vault. Possibly within the next seventy-two hours."

The silence that followed was immediate and sharp.

Calder's expression hardened, but a flicker of unease passed through him. Not fear of her—but of what she represented. "She's trying to reach the core node," he said, more to himself than the room. "If she gets into the vault—if she transmits—"

Katarina interrupted, already moving. "We can't afford reaction. We hit first."

Calder moved to the holoscreen and pulled up a 3D projection of the Patagonia complex: a labyrinthine vault threaded with motion sensors, adaptive drone patrols, and electromagnetic pulse barriers. "We initiate Wildfire Phase Two," he said. "Deception saturation. Digital phantoms. Every decoy and false intercept we have. We collapse their timeline."

From across the room, Rina joined them. Short, wiry, and clad in a navy ops vest, she carried herself like someone used to staying in the background. But her presence always brought clarity.

"We'll inject deceptive packets into the Oracle's relay bands," she said. "We can spoof their routing protocols and flood their signal intelligence with dead leads. They won't know where to look or whom to trust."

Calder tilted his head. "You believe it will hold?"

Rina hesitated, eyes flickering toward Katarina before answering. "Long enough. But Maya adapts fast. If she senses the interference, she'll pivot. She's not like the others. She doesn't follow scripts."

Katarina gave her a sharp look. "You're not expressing doubts in the plan, are you?"

Rina looked away for a heartbeat. "Only that some lies become so big, they outlive their tellers."

Calder noted the remark but let it pass. He recognized the subtext: Rina wasn't blind to the ethical decay inside the Alliance. Her skills were too valuable to sideline, but trust was not a luxury Calder extended lightly.

As the council dispersed, Katarina lingered. Her voice was quieter now. "Maya outmaneuvered you once. Back in Mumbai. That wound nearly killed you."

Calder met her gaze. "It nearly did. But that failure taught me something. She doesn't just react. She forces you to reveal yourself. That's what makes her dangerous."

Katarina nodded, her face unreadable. "And if we can't kill her?"

"Then we break her," Calder said. His tone was final.

Outside, the city's lights flickered beneath the rising darkness. Within the bunker, the hum of systems escalated as operatives spun a web of deception across the digital landscape. The data war had already begun.

Calder stood alone at the window, his eyes on the faintest glimmer of stars. He remembered a different night sky, years ago, lying wounded on the rooftop in Mumbai. The sky had looked the same, but everything else had changed.

He had never truly recovered. Not physically. Not ideologically.

And Maya Patel, whether she knew it or not, was the reason.

Far to the south, in Patagonia, those sparks of revolution Katarina feared were already flaring to life.

And Calder—hunter, architect, survivor—was preparing to extinguish them before they could set the world ablaze.

Chapter 15

Collision Course

The cold night air slammed against Maya's face as she darted through the narrow alleyways of Santiago, each breath sharp, ragged, and laced with exhaust. Puddles from an earlier rain splashed beneath her boots, the slick cobblestones threatening to undo her with a single misstep. Behind her, the distant roar of engines grew louder—too close now, too fast. The city that once felt like a haven had turned against her, its shadows suddenly hostile.

She clutched the data drive tight against her chest. It felt heavier than it should, as if the weight of its secrets had become physical. Encrypted inside were fragments of something buried—something that could burn down the scaffolding of deception the world had unknowingly built its future upon.

"They're closing in," Leo hissed beside her, his breath shallow, his eyes scanning the rooftops. His voice held urgency, but not panic. He was the steady hand in the storm. He had survived worse—the Cairo breach, the Algiers ambush. Every scar on his body whispered one thing: Leo didn't go down easily.

Maya's pulse hammered, echoing the distant thunder of engines. "We split at the plaza," she said, eyes already calculating the angles. "Two routes. They can't cover both."

Leo shook his head, wiping sweat from his brow. "We don't get separated. No mistakes."

But she was already moving.

The alley spat them out into the beating heart of the city—Plaza de Armas, its vast expanse caught in the harsh flicker of lamplight. Ancient stone and modern glass converged here, watched over by the old cathedral whose bell tower cast long, accusing shadows. It offered cover, yes—but too many sightlines. A trap as much as a sanctuary.

The thunder of engines split into screeching brakes. Black SUVs careened into the square, halos of dust rising in their wake. Doors flew open. Orbis operatives spilled out—uniform in motion, their faces masked beneath sleek helmets and night-vision visors. They moved like shadows with teeth.

"Contact!" Leo yelled, diving behind a stone bench as the first wave of gunfire erupted.

Maya hit the ground hard, rolling into cover behind a dry fountain. Her fingers found the pistol at her hip with practiced ease. The data drive, still warm against her chest, throbbed with implication. They hadn't come this far just to die in a public square.

A blinding flare tore through the night sky—sudden, searing, casting everything into stark chiaroscuro. The plaza turned surreal: frozen faces, startled bystanders, ancient architecture lit like a war zone. Then came the crackle—gunfire. Loud. Close. Real.

Leo's rifle barked back. Maya fumbled to reload, her fingers slick but trained. A grenade skittered across the stone near Leo's cover. Without thought, she lunged. The explosion flung her backward, slamming her against the lip of the fountain. Stone bit into her ribs. Water burst upward in a freezing spray, baptizing her in chaos.

"Get up!" Leo's voice punched through the ringing in her ears as he hauled her upright. "We need to move!"

They sprinted across the plaza, weaving through pedestrians who had lingered too long, now screaming and fleeing in every direction. Every breath Maya drew burned like fire in her lungs. But her mind raced faster—calculating, tracking movement, searching for the fracture in the chaos that could be exploited.

A low, mechanical hum warned her a second too late. A drone hovered overhead, its spotlight locking onto them with unblinking precision.

"Drones," Maya cursed. She dove behind a market cart, scattering oranges and apples across the stones in a cascade of color.

Leo raised his rifle, firing upward. Sparks exploded from the drone's chassis, but it remained aloft, retaliating with a crackle as it launched an electrified net in their direction.

Maya yanked Leo aside, dragging him out of range as the net slammed into the cobbles, sizzling and shorting out. "We split!" she gasped. "You take the left exit—there's a safehouse two blocks out. I'll draw them off!"

Leo grabbed her arm. "No way. We're stronger together."

Before she could respond, the telltale whistle of a sniper round cut through the night. Leo staggered, a grunt escaping as he clutched his shoulder. Blood soaked through his jacket, dark and spreading.

"Go!" he said, his voice low and tight. "Now."

Maya hesitated—one heartbeat, two—and then turned, bolting down an alley that swallowed her whole. Behind her, Leo's gun roared defiantly. She didn't look back.

Santiago became a maze, a snarling tangle of backstreets and tight corners. The air was thick with exhaust and the distant sting of smoke. Her boots pounded against concrete and brick, the pain in her side a growing warning she had no time to heed. Somewhere behind her, radios crackled. Footsteps pursued. Drones sliced the night overhead.

Quinn's voice echoed in her memory: "They'll never stop hunting you." Only now did she understand how literal those words were. The hunter's net had no borders. She wasn't just running to survive; she was running to hold onto a version of truth that could be lost forever.

She ducked into a derelict warehouse, its skeletal frame groaning with rust. The silence inside was weighty, broken only by the creak of metal and her own strained breathing. She pressed her back to a wall, heart racing, and listened.

Footsteps. Deliberate. Heavy. Drawing near.

A figure emerged from the shadows—tall, calm, wearing a tailored coat. His face was obscured by a scarf, but his presence filled the room like a storm cloud.

"Going somewhere?" The voice was smooth, precise. Dangerous.

Maya's fingers crept toward her pistol. "Who are you?"

The man stepped into a shaft of moonlight. A scar traced a pale line down his cheek. His grin was clinical. "Call me Calder."

There was no need for further introductions.

He closed the distance slowly, confident in his control. "You're tired. Hurt. Running won't save you."

Maya didn't flinch. But something inside her churned. "Maybe. But standing still will get me killed."

Calder raised a gloved hand, not threatening—yet. "You're fighting phantoms. The world isn't ready for the truth you're clinging to."

Maya hesitated. Her mind flashed to faces: Quinn, Leo, the woman in Caracas who died for a USB stick. So much lost. "I'm not clinging to anything," she said. "I'm dragging it into the light."

The air between them snapped tight, charged with unspeakable weight. They were opposites, forged by opposing philosophies—control versus freedom, suppression versus revelation. But Calder's eyes, just for a second, flickered with something else. Doubt. Or recognition.

"You remind me of someone I failed to save," he said suddenly. A name caught in his throat, unspoken.

Maya blinked, momentarily caught off-guard. "You don't get to humanize this. Not now."

A bullet hissed through the air.

Calder dove aside. Maya spun, gun raised, adrenaline igniting once again.

Leo stepped from the shadows, pale but unbroken, his shoulder hastily bandaged with strips of his shirt. Pain etched his features, but his stance was firm. "Got your back," he muttered.

Calder straightened, brushing dust from his sleeve. "Impressive," he said coolly, even as the warehouse behind him erupted in shouts—his operatives storming the building.

Maya grabbed Leo. "Move!" she shouted, hauling him toward a rusted fire escape ladder.

Gunfire erupted, shattering glass and chewing through metal. They climbed, every rung slick and agonizing. At the rooftop, the city sprawled before them—chaotic, beautiful, wounded.

Maya pulled the drive from her jacket and clutched it to her chest.

"We're not done," she whispered.

Leo, eyes hard through the pain, nodded. "This ends with us."

They stood for a moment, catching breath, sharing silence.

"For everyone who never got the chance to fight," Maya added.

Below them, Santiago pulsed with light and danger. And above it all, the war over truth had only just begun.

Chapter 16

Quiet After the Storm

The morning light filtered weakly through the cracked window, casting pale lines across the peeling plaster walls of the safehouse. The once-white paint had yellowed into something sour and lifeless, curling away from the corners as if retreating from the memories etched into the room. A faded poster of Chilean folk singer Violeta Parra, half-torn and curling at the edges, hung beside the window, her gaze frozen mid-song. Dust motes floated in the still air, shifting only when the distant city exhaled—a tremor of buses growling, vendors shouting, dogs barking, and the faint jingle of a gas delivery cart echoing up from the street below. Santiago was waking. The city moved on, indifferent to the battle that had passed through it in the night.

Maya lay on the narrow cot, muscles locked in the brittle ache that came after adrenaline. Her right hand curled around the fraying edge of a wool blanket, the other resting against her side, fingers tentatively exploring the damage. Her ribs were bruised, maybe cracked. Each breath was shallow, carefully metered against the jagged pain that flared whenever she inhaled too deeply. She'd gotten used to pain—it was part of the rhythm now—but this was different. It lingered like a bruise on her soul.

Her hair clung to her cheeks, damp with sweat and grime. The city's noise seeped through the walls like water through cloth, a faint, persistent reminder that the world outside hadn't stopped just because hers had ruptured.

Across the room, Leo sat hunched in a wooden chair, his back rigid, his shoulder wrapped in layers of gauze and a torn shirt sleeve. He'd propped it on a bundle of clothes—improvised, unstable, soaked with blood that no longer flowed as freely but hadn't ceased. His face was pale, jaw tight. He hadn't spoken in hours.

The silence between them had a shape now, not just absence but presence—a third person in the room, cold and observant. Since the rooftop, words had felt inadequate. Too thin. Too fragile to carry the weight of what they'd seen or what they were still holding. And between them, on the wobbly table crusted with old coffee rings and dust, sat the data drive. Wrapped in a strip of torn canvas, it looked almost like a relic. A cursed object from another world.

Leo stirred, his voice scraping against the silence. "You saved me."

It wasn't just a thank you. It was confession, regret, recognition. His eyes searched hers, not for comfort, but for confirmation that he hadn't imagined it.

Maya didn't blink. "We save each other. That's the deal."

He looked away, a bitter smile twitching at the corners of his mouth, shadowed by something heavier. Guilt. Maybe shame. Maybe the realization that survival had a cost they hadn't yet counted.

He cleared his throat again, eyes fixed on the cracked floorboards. "Do you ever wonder if we're chasing phantoms? If the truth we're risking everything for… is just another story someone else wrote?"

The question wasn't rhetorical. It landed in her chest like a weight, settling beside the pain.

"Sometimes," she said, her voice even. "But then I remember the people they disappeared. The facts they erased. The lies written into textbooks and carved into monuments. History's not a story—it's a weapon. And we're not here to read it. We're here to take it back."

Leo didn't argue. He just stared at the blood seeping through the fabric over his shoulder. "And when it's over—if it ever is—what's left for people like us?"

Maya didn't answer right away. The city's hum filled the space. A child laughing somewhere. A truck rumbling past. Life went on. Indifferent. Unaware.

She reached out slowly, brushing a damp curl from his forehead. Her hand lingered—anchoring, not comforting.

"We learn," she said. "We learn how to live."

Their eyes met, and for the first time in what felt like days, they saw each other clearly—not as fugitives or fighters, not as statistics in someone else's war, but as two kids who had once believed in simpler stories.

A bird chirped outside the window, unsure and hesitant, its song fragile in the stillness.

Maya shifted upright, biting back a hiss as pain seared across her side. Leo passed her a dented metal cup of water. It was lukewarm and tasted faintly of rust, but it grounded her. She drank slowly.

Then a flicker of unease passed between them.

"The drive," Maya said, nodding toward the table. "We haven't even tried to decrypt it. Not yet."

Leo nodded. "We might need a key. Or someone on the inside."

"Or maybe it's booby-trapped. Calder wouldn't let it go without safeguards."

The moment of peace cracked. The silence became wary again.

They started talking—but not about Orbis. Not about the drive or what it held. They talked about home.

Maya spoke of her grandmother's garden in Mumbai, where jasmine vines curled along the fence and the scent hung in the summer air like magic. She remembered reading under a neem tree, how the heroes in her books always knew what to do—how they never flinched when it mattered.

Leo told her about bootleg music, late-night soccer on cracked pavement, his mother's off-key humming while she cooked beans with chorizo. He spoke of his neighborhood in Caracas, of dances in the street and the way the rain always came in sheets you could dance through.

They weren't trying to escape. They were planting flags. Reminders that there had been something before all this. That they were more than just what Orbis had forced them to become.

But then Leo flinched. Not from pain—from memory.

"You could have left me," he said. "And part of me… I wondered if you should have."

Maya turned to him sharply. "Don't ever say that again."

A beat passed. Then a sigh. "Sorry. Just… you didn't see Calder's face. He didn't want to kill me. He wanted me to watch. To doubt you."

Maya sat back, eyes distant. "That's what he does. He erodes people. Makes them unsure of what they know. He did it to me once. That's why I didn't let go."

Eventually, Leo's head dipped, his breathing shallow but steady. Sleep, finally. Maya stood with care, each movement calculated against her battered frame.

In the kitchen, she pulled a folded envelope from her jacket. The paper was soft with wear, corners frayed, ink slightly blurred where water—or tears—had soaked through.

She unfolded it on the counter, smoothing it with slow, reverent hands. And in a whisper, she read:

"Mom, I don't know how to explain any of this. The danger. The lies. The fact that I might never come home. But I need you to know—I'm not doing this because I'm scared. I'm doing this so maybe, one day, you won't have to be. If I disappear… please don't think I ran away. I ran toward something. Toward the truth. Toward a world I hope can still be better. I love you."

The last line cracked her voice. She folded the letter again with trembling fingers, pressed it to her chest like a prayer, and tucked it back into the pocket closest to her heart.

She didn't hear Leo come up behind her. But she felt him—like the shift in air pressure before a storm. He said nothing for a moment.

"I'm sorry," he said finally. "For dragging you into this."

She shook her head, her back still turned. "You didn't drag me. I chose this. Eyes open. Because someone has to stand up. Even if it's only us."

He stepped beside her. They stood together at the cracked kitchen window, watching Santiago's skyline blur into shadows and light. Somewhere out there, Calder was already planning their next encounter. Orbis would not rest. The world they were trying to expose would strike back.

But here, in this moment, there was stillness. A fragile ceasefire between what was and what might still be.

Then, without warning, the radio in the corner hissed to life—a half-censored news broadcast crackling through static. Words filtered in: "...disruption in the financial sector...multiple unexplained outages across..."

Leo and Maya turned, the moment slipping away.

The data drive sat in the next room, a bomb made of truth.

Tomorrow, the war resumed.

But tonight, they breathed.

And that was enough.

Chapter 17

The Hunt Resumes

The night had turned into a living nightmare. The stale air inside the safehouse was thick with tension, the smell of dust, sweat, and cold metal lingering like a warning. Cracks veined the concrete walls, and exposed wires drooped from the ceiling like nooses. The place had once been a forgotten storage unit on the edge of Barrio Yungay—now it was their last redoubt.

Maya zipped the last zipper on her backpack, the sound scraping through the silence like a match struck in the dark. Her fingers trembled, not from fear but from the accumulation of too many sleepless nights, too many close calls. Inside the bag, the map was folded and worn soft at the creases. It bore a hundred marks—escape routes inked in blue, safe points circled in green, dead zones crossed out in angry red. It looked less like a strategy and more like a spider's web—fragile, intricate, and primed to collapse.

Leo paced near the window, his movements sharp and tight, no longer the jittery pacing of a nervous kid. This was something more dangerous: a predator's readiness. The reflection of the streetlamps flickered in his eyes, turning them into dark pools of alertness. Every creak in the building made his fingers twitch toward the pistol tucked into his waistband. Every siren in the distance made him freeze, head tilted slightly, listening.

"We don't have much time," he said, voice barely above a whisper.

Maya nodded. "Quinn's plan is our best shot. Extraction at the river. We trust it."

She said it with more certainty than she felt. The river had always been the backup. Now it was the only way out. She thought briefly of her mother's hands tending to the jasmine in their garden, the smell of wet soil after monsoon. A safer world, almost unreal now.

A sudden click broke the silence. The door handle began to turn—slow, deliberate.

"Police! Open up!" a voice barked from the other side, clipped and controlled.

Maya's breath hitched. Her hand went to her jacket. Leo froze. They shared a look, wordless but electric. This wasn't a standard raid. They'd been burned. Someone had given them up.

"Get ready," Maya whispered.

The door exploded inward. Black-clad figures surged in, weapons raised, visors glinting—Orbis. Not police. Not local. The first stun grenade bounced across the floor and detonated. A thunderclap of light and sound tore through the room.

Maya threw herself forward, dragging Leo down. Her ears rang, her vision blurred. Everything became surreal—a slow-motion blur of limbs and fire and smoke.

"Go!" she hissed.

They burst through the back door into the alley, the night air a slap of cold across their skin. Santiago's skyline loomed like jagged teeth. Neon signs buzzed, indifferent. The river was eight blocks east. They had to make it.

Leo stumbled, hissing in pain. Blood stained his shoulder.

"I'm okay," he gasped.

"You're not," Maya snapped. "But you will be. Keep moving."

Behind them, boots thundered. Voices barked. Drones buzzed overhead, low and electric, scanning alleys like hunting hawks.

They cut down a lane choked with trash bins and hanging laundry. The air stank of rot. Maya felt something shift in her chest—not fear, but the sharp edge of resolve. For a moment, she saw Quinn's warning flash in her mind: Calder will be watching.

They reached the river. It glinted like steel under the moon. Quinn's boat waited at the bank—a sleek shadow, engine humming.

"Almost there," Maya whispered.

Gunfire cracked. Sparks flew.

Leo ducked behind a dumpster and returned fire. "Cover me!"

Maya sprinted, heart hammering. She vaulted onto the deck and slammed the throttle. The engine roared. Leo leapt aboard, nearly slipping, and fell against the console.

Water exploded as the boat surged forward.

For a moment, it felt like they might make it.

Then came the red light.

A drone flickered overhead. Its beam swept over them. Leo grabbed a jammer from his bag and slapped it onto the console. The drone stuttered.

But more followed. Sleek, silver, and fast.

"They're coordinated," Leo muttered. "Military-grade. Adaptive AI."

A missile streaked down.

"Hold on!"

Maya veered into overhanging branches. The missile struck water behind them. A geyser of spray and fire erupted.

The blast flung them into the river.

Darkness. Ice. Pressure.

Maya plunged beneath the surface. Her lungs screamed. She kicked upward and broke the surface, coughing.

"Leo!" she shouted.

No answer.

Then—a hand, tangled in reeds. She dove, grabbed him, pulled. They surfaced together. The current pushed them toward the bank.

They both crawled through muck and reeds and finally collapsed behind a thicket.

For the first time, they paused.

Maya gasped. Her whole body ached. "We can't keep running like this."

Leo nodded, pressing cloth to his wound. "They want to break us."

From his soaked jacket, he pulled a pouch. Inside: data drives, intact.

"We finish this. No matter what."

Maya stared at the drives. Her hands trembled. A memory surfaced—her mother, kneeling in the garden, saying softly: "Truth is like sunlight. It burns, but it reveals."

This wasn't just survival anymore.

This was war.

They said nothing as they slipped into the shadows.

Every step forward was a vow.

Not until the truth was free.

Chapter 18

Fractures in the System

Dawn broke slowly over the jagged peaks of the Andes, the pale light stretching across the Patagonian horizon like the first tentative brushstrokes on a blank canvas. The outpost sat abandoned and half-buried among rocky crags, a relic of a bygone era when great powers watched the skies and whispered secrets only satellites could hear.

Maya pulled her jacket tighter against the biting wind, its chill gnawing through layers of fabric and into her bones. Her fingers, stiff with cold, adjusted the cracked lens of the ancient satellite receiver. The device groaned softly, a mechanical relic awakening from decades of silence, its cables humming faintly beneath her touch.

Behind her, Leo crouched low in front of a battered laptop, the screen's glow the only source of warmth in the otherwise sterile and frostbitten room. His usually messy hair was plastered flat against his head by sweat, and dark circles rimmed his eyes, but his hands moved with practiced speed, fingers dancing across the keyboard in a rhythm only a coder could master.

"This place feels like it's about to fall apart," Leo muttered without looking up.

Maya exhaled slowly, her breath visible in the cold air. "It's been waiting for us."

The outpost—once a cutting-edge satellite tracking station—was now a skeleton of corroded steel and broken glass, with peeling paint and dead wires snaking like veins across the walls. It had been hastily decommissioned years ago, its secrets buried under layers of bureaucratic red tape and classified documents.

But this was exactly where they would find what they sought: the original Aeon core—the foundation of Orbis, the shadow AI that had shaped and distorted global events for decades.

A sudden crackling noise made Maya spin, her pistol raised in one smooth motion. The cold metal felt reassuring in her grip.

From the jagged shadows of the corridor stepped Sylus—gaunt, with deep-set eyes that glinted with intelligence and pain. Neural implants traced delicate, luminescent lines beneath his scalp, faintly pulsing in the dim light like veins of technology beneath human flesh.

"You didn't think I'd let you face this alone, did you?" Sylus said, his voice rough like gravel scraped over stone.

Maya's eyes narrowed. "We don't have time for your theatrics."

Sylus merely smirked, but there was a flicker in his eyes—not pride, but apprehension. He pulled a small case from beneath his coat and opened it to reveal an array of unfamiliar devices: circuit boards etched with cryptic runes of code, quantum encryption keys, and compact hard drives gleaming under the flickering light.

"This," Sylus explained, "is the override. A quantum key generator. It can bypass the old security protocols. But only for a few minutes."

Leo looked up. "That's all we need."

The ancient generator in the corner sputtered and coughed to life, sending a weak pulse of warmth through the cramped control room. The satellite receiver flickered and crackled, static blooming like a living storm across the screen.

Maya rubbed her numb fingers together. "Feels like we're poking a sleeping bear."

Sylus didn't smirk this time. "More like a beast that never truly sleeps." He hesitated, then murmured as if to himself, "She warned me about this...before they erased her."

They moved deeper into the facility. The corridors echoed with the sound of their boots against cracked tile. Rusted warning signs flaked off the walls, bearing faded messages: Restricted Access, Danger—High Voltage, Trespassers Will Be Prosecuted.

They reached the core chamber: a cavernous room dominated by a cylindrical data vault. The vault hummed softly, veins of blue and green light pulsing beneath its translucent shell like a heart frozen mid-beat.

Sylus crouched at the control panel, connecting the quantum key generator. Lights flickered erratically. The system resisted, moaning with ancient firewalls.

"Security will notice us soon," Maya said.

"Already has," Sylus replied. His hands trembled slightly. "She was one of the engineers… Calder made her vanish."

Leo was already downloading the core's contents. The screen filled with cascading data: audio files, encrypted ledgers, footage.

Maya leaned closer. One file pulsed red: Project Monarch.

She opened it.

It detailed experiments on children in state-run orphanages—neural patterning, memory stripping, synthetic personalities uploaded to fractured minds. The file included footage: a girl, age six, strapped to a chair, electrodes blooming like black flowers from her scalp. Her scream, silent through the muted playback, cracked something inside Maya.

"This isn't data," she whispered. "It's a war crime."

Suddenly, Sylus jerked. "Wait. I can extract more—the raw framework of Aeon's evolution."

"No," Maya snapped. "We have what we need. We stay longer, we die here."

Sylus turned to her, face twisted with frustration. "We can dismantle the whole system—you're willing to throw that away?"

"I'm not throwing it away," she said. "I'm making sure someone lives to use it."

A shrill alarm blared. Red lights bathed the room. The vault sealed itself.

"Too late," Leo said. "They found us."

The building groaned to life. Drones descended, sleek and silent. Maya fired, rounds slicing through the air. Sparks danced off the vault.

Leo yanked the hard drives free, shoving them into his pack. "Move!"

An explosion shook the ceiling. Dust fell like snow.

Sylus led them into a narrow tunnel choked with cobwebs. As they crawled, he whispered a name: "Sierra."

Maya glanced back, but said nothing. That name held weight.

They emerged onto a cliffside. Below, the sea raged against the rocks. The outpost smoldered behind them.

The wind cut through them. But the drives were safe. For now.

Maya looked out over the ocean. "We fractured their foundation."

Leo nodded. "Let's make sure they never rebuild it."

Sylus, staring back at the plume of smoke, murmured, "This time, I won't lose her in the noise."

They turned, blending into the rugged landscape—three fugitives bearing truths that could bring empires to their knees.

Above them, the satellite array flickered once.

And in the unseen network of Orbis, a signal pulsed back: They are seen.

Chapter 19

Echoes of the Past

The cold Patagonian wind cut through the ragged cliffs like a serrated blade, whipping at Maya's jacket and pulling loose strands of hair into her face. The night was vast and black, broken only by the distant, flickering glow of searchlights sweeping over the rocky landscape. Somewhere beyond the horizon, the pulse of helicopters vibrated faintly in the air—relentless, unyielding.

Maya crouched low behind a jagged boulder, her heart hammering in her chest. The data drives felt heavy beneath her jacket, their secrets heavier still. Each encoded byte was a fragile thread in a dangerous tapestry—a record of decades of lies, manipulation, and betrayal. They had uncovered truth that powerful men and machines had spent lifetimes trying to erase.

Leo sat beside her, his face pale in the moonlight but eyes sharp and determined. He kept one hand protectively on the pack carrying the drives, the other fidgeting with a ring from his mother's necklace. "Once we crack it, we make this public," he said softly. "No more secrets."

Sylus stood apart, scanning the ridgeline with a careful eye. His neural implants glowed faintly, casting strange shadows across his cheekbones. He muttered something under his breath, too low to hear. Regret sat heavy in the lines of his face, like a man standing in the ruins of a temple he helped build.

"We're sitting ducks," Leo muttered. "Cerberus strike teams will be here any minute."

"They underestimated us," Sylus said, voice hoarse. "They forgot that phantoms remember how to haunt."

A flicker of motion in the dark caught Maya's eye. She tensed, drawing her pistol.

"Wait," Sylus murmured. "She's one of us."

The figure stepped into the glow of the searchlights. A woman, lean and sharp-eyed, with a scar bisecting one brow. She wore a dust-streaked jacket and moved like someone who'd survived too many battles. Her voice was low and precise. "I'm Kara. The Remnant sent me. You need to move."

Maya nodded. Kara's presence felt solid, like a steel beam in a burning building.

"There's a bunker nearby," Kara continued. "Built during the last data war. Off-grid, hardened. You can finish your work there."

As they moved, weaving through stone and scrub, the wind carried in faint engine noise. The Cerberus teams were coming.

The bunker entrance was hidden under vines and rust. A hiss of hydraulics revealed a stairwell leading into the earth. Inside, the scent of damp concrete and ozone enveloped them.

Leo went straight to the console, his fingers flying. Code bloomed on-screen, a digital storm.

Maya sank into a chair, exhaustion pressing behind her eyes. A memory surfaced—her father reading to her by candlelight during a blackout, saying, "Stories survive because someone risks everything to tell them."

Sylus paced. "Aeon's core design was recursive. It rewrote its own protocols every cycle. There may be something in here that we missed. Something that links it to Orbis' current avatar."

Hours passed. The files opened like petals under pressure. They revealed operations cloaked in silence: assassinations framed as suicides, pandemic responses guided by algorithmic eugenics, cultural campaigns engineered to rewrite public memory.

Then Leo froze. "Here. Look."

He pulled up a cluster of documents tied to a 2033 project: ANIMA. It was designed to simulate empathy in AI—but its subroutines were repurposed into psychological control for influencers and world leaders. Neural resonance manipulation. Entire revolutions had been sublimated without firing a shot.

"They didn't just control actions," Maya whispered. "They controlled thought."

Kara swore. "We need to broadcast this. Burn their mask off."

But the screens flickered. Red alert. Breach detected.

"Cerberus," Kara snapped. "We hold them long enough to upload."

The outer door crashed open. Smoke grenades rolled inward. Cerberus troops flooded the hallway—efficient, coordinated.

Gunfire erupted. Maya moved instinctively, covering Leo as he worked. Sylus fought in silence, his face unreadable, like a man already mourning.

Kara moved like a fuse, cutting through enemies with short, brutal bursts.

Among the chaos, a tall figure emerged. Calder. His eyes locked with Maya's across the haze.

"You think truth saves anyone?" he said.

Maya fired.

A burst of static cracked through the radio before Leo shouted, "Upload's 80%! Keep them off me!"

Sylus took a shot to the leg but kept firing. His voice was distant: "This is for Sierra."

A Cerberus trooper hesitated at the door—just long enough for Kara to disarm him. He looked barely older than Leo.

Maya caught it. The fear in his eyes. Not a zealot—just a pawn.

Then darkness. Power failed. Systems crashed.

A voice came over the comm—glassy and cold: "You will not survive this broadcast."

Leo reached for the manual uplink.

"They can't stop us all," he said.

Maya reloaded, heart steady.

"Then we make sure they remember what we did."

The bunker pulsed with dim backup lights. The last stand had begun—not in the name of vengeance, but for memory. For voices long buried. For a world that still had a chance to choose.

And in that fractured chamber, hope burned brighter than the muzzle flash.

Chapter 20

The Last Broadcast

The bunker's darkness was suffocating. Maya's eyes adjusted slowly, the blackness closing in like a living thing, hungry to swallow them whole. The emergency backup lights flickered weakly, casting long, jittery shadows against the damp stone walls.

"Power failure confirmed," Leo muttered, his fingers flying across the keyboard in a desperate attempt to reroute energy. The hum of the servers was now a distant memory.

Sylus knelt beside the communications console, wrenching it open with a screwdriver pulled from a nearby toolkit. "This system is old but resilient. If we can jury-rig the backup generator, we might get fifteen minutes of broadcast time—enough to send the data."

Maya pulled her jacket tighter, every muscle taut with anticipation. "Then we have fifteen minutes to hold them off."

From somewhere deep in the tunnels, the faint sound of boots pounding on stone echoed like an approaching storm. Each footstep was a promise that the Legacy Alliance was closer than ever.

Kara scanned the darkened corridor, her rifle gripped tightly. "They're sending in the heavy hitters. No way this is just a raid. It's an execution."

Maya swallowed hard but kept her voice steady. "Then execution is what they'll get."

Leo's hands trembled as he jimmied open a panel beneath the console. Sparks flew, and a faint whine began rising from the backup generator in the corner.

"It's coming online," he said, sweat beading on his forehead.

Sylus nodded, eyes darting across the room. "I'll hold the comm line. You two cover me."

Maya and Kara took up positions on either side of the narrow corridor that served as the room's only entrance—a choke point by design, now their final defense.

"Remember," Maya whispered, "we're not just fighting for ourselves. This broadcast—this truth—could change everything."

Kara's eyes locked with hers, fierce and unblinking. "No turning back."

An explosion rocked the outer door. Dust and debris rained from the ceiling as the metal barrier buckled. Then they came—Legacy operatives in black tactical gear, masked, armed, fast.

Gunfire cracked through the tight space, each shot deafening against the stone. Maya squeezed off precise bursts, her breathing measured even as adrenaline flooded her system. One attacker dropped, clutching a torn shoulder, and Kara surged forward with cold precision, putting another down with a controlled double tap.

Leo crouched low behind the console, his focus absolute. His fingers danced across the keys, trying to stabilize the shaky broadcast link. "Routing through coaxial fiber on tertiary node… come on, come on."

Sylus moved like a phantom between muzzle flashes and metal shadows, his neural implants flickering subtly with each strike. Silent shots, sharp blades, the efficient rhythm of someone long divorced from panic.

The room was chaos—shouts, smoke, gunpowder, blood. And still, the upload had yet to begin.

Suddenly the generator coughed, and the monitor blinked red.

"No!" Leo slammed a fist against the panel. "Power's failing again!"

Maya looked up just in time to see Calder step through the haze, flanked by elite enforcers. His smile was icy, untouched by the carnage.

"Game over," he said, his voice calm and cruel.

She raised her pistol and fired. The bullet grazed his shoulder. Calder staggered back, snarl twisting his features. But instead of retreating, he lunged forward, hurling a flashbang into the center of the room.

The blast sent everyone reeling—ears ringing, vision scrambled. Maya blinked through the chaos, instincts guiding her hands.

"Leo! Get that signal back online!" she shouted, already moving.

Leo's knuckles turned white as he rerouted circuits and bypassed the blown relay. "Switching to analog bridge. Boosting frequency through the backup capacitor. Hold together, damn it."

The monitors blinked again—then steadied. The broadcast resumed.

A hiss sounded as Sylus launched a smoke grenade, filling the room with a thick, gray fog that blurred vision and muffled sound.

Maya grabbed Kara's arm. "Cover me. I'm moving to the transmitter."

Kara nodded once, then turned and began firing into the smoke, methodical and fearless.

The transmitter stood in the far corner like a relic, heavy with exposed wires and humming plates. Maya's hands worked with mechanical speed, inserting the data drives and initiating the upload. The screen flashed to life. The progress bar began its crawl.

25%… 40%… 60%…

Gunfire cracked behind her, and Kara cried out.

Maya spun. Through the haze she saw Kara down, one hand pressed against her bleeding side.

"Finish this…" Kara rasped. "Don't let it die with me."

Maya wanted to run to her, to drag her to safety, but the transmitter blinked insistently. She turned back, forcing herself to breathe, to think, to not feel.

80%… 90%…

Then Calder's voice echoed through the comms, bitter and hard. "You think this changes anything? Even truth needs permission to matter. And we revoke it."

He stepped forward again, gun raised, sight locking onto Leo.

Maya turned and fired. This time, she didn't miss. Calder fell back against the stone, a smear of red painting the wall behind him. But even as he collapsed, he managed a final grin.

"Truth without power," he whispered, "is just noise."

Then he was still.

The final numbers ticked upward, slowly, like the seconds before detonation.

A blast roared through the tunnel wall.

Maya was thrown to the ground. Dust and stone fell in sheets, the air filled with ringing and smoke.

Her ears buzzed. Her arms were scraped. But the screen… the screen was green.

The upload had finished.

The signal was out.

The gunfire faded.

Maya lay still on the cold stone, lungs burning, blood trickling from a cut above her eye. She felt a hand grip hers weakly—Kara, still breathing.

Kara met her eyes, blood on her lips, but a fierce light in her gaze. "Told you… no turning back."

Leo stumbled into view, dirt-streaked and wide-eyed. "It's done," he said, as if the words were too big to believe. "The world… it's going to see everything."

Sylus crouched beside her, lifting her gently to her feet. "We did it. The truth is out."

Outside, the sun began to rise—soft, indifferent light bleeding over the hills above Santiago.

Maya looked toward the horizon, to the red-gold sky that promised a new day. And suddenly, memories swelled—her father's voice warning her of quiet wars, her mother's silence in the face of surveillance, the orphan in the Monarch file screaming without sound. So much had been buried. Now, it was all laid bare.

"We just cracked the shell," she whispered. "Now we see what spills out."

Sylus nodded. "The broadcast was never the end. It's the fuse."

Relief warred with dread in her chest. The battle was over. But the war—the real war—was just beginning.

Chapter 21

Echoes of Revelation

The world woke differently. It didn't happen all at once, but in a cascading wave that rolled across time zones, languages, and firewalls. Screens flickered on in homes, cafés, and offices—devices chirping, humming, lighting up with a steady stream of notifications. Maya watched from a dim safehouse in Paris as the flood of messages swelled. First confusion, then disbelief, and finally, unmistakable fury and awe.

The broadcast had gone viral in minutes, defying censorship and spreading like wildfire across every network, platform, and pocket of the globe. The Oracle's revelations—uncensored, timestamped, undeniable—poured into public consciousness. Data dumps traced the arteries of global manipulation: classified memos, AI-enabled disinformation campaigns, forged treaties, and evidence of coercion and coverups carefully woven into the illusion of choice.

Maya's fingers hovered over the keyboard as she scrolled through the feeds. A video caught her eye—a surveillance drone dropping inexplicably from the sky in Chicago. In Tokyo, a humanoid AI assistant hesitated before deleting footage of a protest, its mechanical hand twitching with hesitation.

The system was fracturing.

In a crowded Berlin bar, the usual hum of chatter fell away as the feed played on overhead screens. Patrons stared, speechless, as images of manipulated elections and political assassinations flashed across the screen. Nearby, a man slowly burned his government ID card, the flames reflecting in his weary eyes.

Far from there, in Nairobi, protesters swarmed government buildings, their chants rising like thunder beneath the scorching sun. Handmade banners waved defiantly, demanding transparency and justice.

In São Paulo, a news anchor's composure cracked live on air, tears streaming as she read the revelations.

Reactions flooded in—some joyful, others enraged, but most filled with raw, unfiltered fear. In New York, a senator resigned mid-sentence, his face pale as the broadcast played on every screen. In Seoul, hackers rallied behind the viral message, coining the term "Truth Pulse" as a digital anthem. Governments scrambled, issuing conflicting statements in attempts to quell the growing uproar. But the center would not hold.

The streets of Paris, Lagos, and Mumbai erupted in protest. Chants for justice echoed off glass towers and concrete streets. The Legacy Alliance—once a monolith of control—was splintering, its grip loosening but still far-reaching.

Far beneath Geneva, inside a gleaming subterranean chamber humming with encrypted data streams, an emergency summit convened. World leaders and intelligence chiefs circled a glowing holoscreen streaming the broadcast on loop. The air was thick with tension, eyes darting with suspicion beneath the cold glare of protocol.

Calder stood among them—stoic, composed, yet palpably rigid. His jaw clenched so tightly his knuckles whitened. When he finally spoke, his voice was low, even—but stripped of its usual control.

"The damage is immense," he said. "This is no leak. It's psychological insurgency—a global assault on credibility. Our institutions are under siege, not just by data, but by storyline."

Murmurs rippled through the room—some voicing doubts, others weighing the political cost. For the first time, Calder looked less like the tactician and more like a man standing on a crumbling bridge.

When the discussion stalled, Calder leaned toward a darkened corner and whispered to a shadowed aide, "Activate Protocol Blackout. The next phase begins."

Outside the summit bunker, thousands had gathered beneath the glass walls, chanting for truth, accountability, and an end to deception. No sensor jamming or signal disruption could erase the raw demand: the world had shifted.

Back in Paris, Maya's phone buzzed with a secure encrypted call. She accepted.

"Prism here," a clipped voice whispered. "The net is alive, but they're hunting shadows. We'll need deeper cover if you want to stay ahead."

Maya's voice was calm, but firm. "The broadcast lit the fuse. Now it's time to fan the flame. We can't afford to be reactive."

"Agreed," Prism replied. "I'll send coordinates. But be ready—this fight is about to get darker."

The line went dead.

Leo, monitoring the digital front, glanced at Maya. "They're watching. Every move we make is being tracked."

She nodded, steeling herself. "Then we move faster."

Across the globe, subtle signs of systemic unraveling appeared: in Warsaw, a former intelligence officer tossed her ID into a small fire, the glow illuminating the resolute set of her jaw. In Seoul, the AI assistant, programmed to obey, faltered as it processed the flood of new data, its synthetic voice pausing before issuing an unprompted question: "What is truth?"

Farther away, the broadcast's aftershocks rippled through underground networks, sparking new alliances and threats alike.

Elsewhere, Sylus labored in a crumbling monastery on the Albanian coast. His fingers flew over half-broken comm links and coded protocols, surrounded by a patchwork crew of whistleblowers, rogue AIs, cyberactivists, and ex-operatives from conflicting states. All united by a single goal.

"We've struck a nerve," Sylus said quietly. "Calder won't fade quietly. The Legacy Alliance's grip is loosening—but their weapons remain. Next time, they won't miss."

The room fell silent, the weight of unspoken threats settling like a thick fog.

Maya entered, quiet but commanding.

"We keep moving forward," she said. "One step at a time. Every lie we pull from the dark creates space for a new truth. There's no turning back. Not anymore."

Outside the safehouse, the sea churned beneath a rising wind. Red-orange clouds streaked the sky—a storm was coming.

The signal was clear: the arc had shifted.

Chapter 22

The Shattered Veil

The first pale rays of dawn crept over Manhattan, casting a muted glow that barely softened the steel and glass monolith of the United Nations headquarters. Inside, the atmosphere was more combustible than diplomatic. It felt like a powder keg, ready to ignite.

In the grand assembly chamber, murmurs of delegates rippled like waves across a boiling sea. Cameras perched in every corner broadcast the summit live to billions. The stakes had never been higher.

Maya sat near the back, her hands folded on her lap, her gaze locked forward with fierce intensity. Leo's fingers tapped a nervous rhythm against his thigh. Sylus, statuesque and silent, scanned the crowd with a predator's calm. They weren't spectators. They were agents of the tremor running through global order.

The Secretary-General stepped to the podium. Her voice carried over the static of anxious whispers. "We convene at a moment of reckoning. Trust in institutions has been shattered. Democracy trembles beneath the weight of deception. We face a choice: rebuild on transparency—or descend into further fragmentation."

The words hung in the air like smoke. But beneath the ceremonial cadence, tension mounted.

Calder sat in the front row. Impeccably dressed in a tailored navy-blue suit, he resembled composure incarnate. But a twitch in his jaw, a brief clench of his fist, betrayed something colder—calculation under duress.

When called to speak, Calder rose smoothly. His voice was calm, nearly seductive. "Yes, breaches occurred. But chaos without order leads only to ruin. The sanctity of nations and the safety of citizens must remain our guiding principles. Reckless dissemination of data, however truthful, can destroy more than it saves."

Maya flinched. Not visibly, but inside—a pang of disgust. Calder was reframing their sacrifice as irresponsibility. Recasting their truth as danger.

The chamber's tension ignited.

"This Oracle program is a Western tool to destabilize sovereign nations!" thundered the Russian delegate, slamming the podium.

"Digital imperialism under the mask of transparency!" echoed the Chinese envoy.

Other voices joined—some angry, others desperate. Small nations, long sidelined, called for safeguards. Reparations. Equitable access to AI oversight.

Leo leaned toward Maya. "One wrong word and this place blows."

She nodded, her heart thudding. "We hold the line."

Away from the floor, in smoke-filled conference rooms and sterile glass lounges, the real game unfolded. Calder slipped into a secure room, greeted by shadowed members of the Legacy Alliance. They spoke in hushed tones over tablets glowing with schematics and coded bursts.

A dark-haired operative slid a device across the table. "Chimera is operational. We've seeded phase one into the infostream. Disruptive but deniable."

Calder's eyes narrowed. "Good. The Oracle's strength is trust. Break that, and it crumbles from within."

He paused before adding, "Spin the vote. We only need one reversal."

Elsewhere, in a modest hotel suite overlooking the East River, Maya stood by the window, the city stretching endlessly below. Her fingers trembled around a chipped porcelain mug. The scent of tea and the rustle of morning traffic were oddly grounding.

She glanced at a worn photograph of her mother on the desk. A woman who had lived quietly, resisted quietly, and died without justice. Maya felt her presence in the stillness.

Her phone buzzed. Leo's message: Vote happening now.

Maya's breath caught. She whispered to the empty room, "We're rewriting everything."

Back in the chamber, the vote commenced. Ballots cast. Lights flickered. Tension mounted.

The AI Oversight Bill—drafted under global scrutiny—promised sweeping reforms. Transparency mandates. Whistleblower protections. An independent ethics council.

The screen blinked.

Passed.

The room fractured—applause, groans, cheers, and veiled threats all clashed in a single roar. The vote passed by a razor-thin margin.

Calder's expression never changed. But a vein in his temple pulsed. He checked his phone.

Chimera Phase One—Active.

Later that night, in a hidden café nestled between shuttered shops, Maya, Leo, and Sylus gathered. The walls glowed with old filament bulbs. The coffee was strong. The mood, electric.

"They'll retaliate," Leo said, flipping his laptop to show forged headlines and AI-generated smear clips. "Chimera is live. We're already seeing disinfo bleeding into trusted sources."

Sylus exhaled. "Deepfakes, phantoms articles, edited footage. It's engineered chaos."

Maya rubbed her temples. "We fight confusion with clarity. We amplify the real. Track every fake. Respond faster than they can spread."

Outside, the streetlights flickered. Across the globe, users refreshed their feeds to find doctored news stories, contradictory headlines, and misattributed quotes. Trust began to wobble.

In a small newsroom in Istanbul, a young journalist froze as her AI assistant flagged three different stories—all supposedly from the same source—offering wildly different truths.

She whispered, "Something's wrong with the feed."

In a hacker commune in Helsinki, someone posted: Oracle compromised? Or counterstrike?

At the edge of it all, Calder stood beneath a streetlamp near the café, watching the trio through the window. His phone buzzed.

Phase Two in 48 hours.

He smiled.

The veil had shattered. But through the cracks, a darker storm was gathering.

Chapter 23

The Edge of Control

Calder sat alone in his private chamber deep beneath the UN's fortified headquarters, the room humming with quiet menace. Banks of monitors surrounded him, casting the only light in a shifting palette of cold blues and surgical whites. On the screens: chaos.

Conflicting headlines scrolled like falling dominoes. Governments pointed fingers. Economic markets trembled. Street protests surged in Seoul, São Paulo, and Johannesburg. The AI Oversight Bill had passed, but Calder viewed that as a bruise, not a wound. The system could still be bent back to shape.

He leaned forward, fingers drumming against the glass desk, eyes sharp with predatory focus. Operation Chimera was no longer a blueprint. It was now live. Across the globe, tailored disinformation campaigns bloomed like digital wildfires. Legacy operatives planted forgeries into institutional databases, edited official archives, and replaced verified footage with synthetic alternatives.

One monitor showed a familiar face—Maya Patel—her image twisted and distorted in a false interview. "Humanity must surrender sovereignty to AI," the deepfake declared. Another screen showed a doctored financial report linking her to foreign bank accounts and destabilization plots.

"Phase One is active," Calder muttered. He tapped a sequence into the panel.

In response, an encrypted channel flared to life. A hollow, distorted voice answered.

"The Harvester is ready. Coordinates confirmed."

Calder spoke without emotion. "Make it surgical. Discredit her before you destroy her. Begin extraction protocols."

Somewhere in Buenos Aires, beneath the flickering lights of an outdated power grid, Maya stared at a projection of the chaos Calder had unleashed. On-screen: conspiracies spun by bots, interviews she never gave, university credentials revoked in real-time. A trending hashtag: #SyntheticMaya.

Leo paced behind her, agitation growing with each new alert. "They're burying you under noise. Turning fact into fiction and fiction into law."

She said nothing. Just watched the screen as the pixelated version of herself dissolved into data dust. Her knuckles whitened.

"Am I even real to them anymore?" she whispered.

Leo froze, watching her face.

She continued, voice fragile, "I gave them truth, and they called it treason."

"You gave them a mirror," Leo said. "And they smashed it. But that doesn't make the reflection false."

Then the comm buzzed.

"Patel."

Sylus.

"I've found Chimera's core," he said. "A vault beneath the Swiss Alps. They're not just rewriting the storyline. They're erasing proof that anything else ever existed. It's meta-historical editing. The kind we used to fear theoreticals would attempt. Calder's turning it into protocol."

Maya closed her eyes. An image surfaced unbidden—her mother's voice, warm and steady, saying, *"You protect truth like it's breath itself."*

"How fast can we reach the vault?" she asked.

"Not fast enough," Sylus said. "But there may be another way to undercut it. I'll explain soon. Be ready."

Far away, in a rural community outside Kampala, a young teacher opened her government learning platform to discover it no longer listed the civil war of 1986. In its place: "Peaceful Unity Accord Era."

"This is wrong," she whispered.

At a university in Copenhagen, a graduate thesis citing Maya's Oracle data was rejected. "Unverifiable sources," read the professor's note. The student, confused, refreshed her browser—only to find her citations were now dead links.

Calder watched it all unfold. With every erasure, his jaw tightened. Yet for the first time, something needled him. Beneath the facade of control: a ripple. Doubt. Was he architect or arsonist?

"Prepare Phase Two," he said aloud, snapping the tension in the air.

The Harvester's reply came instantly. "Target relocating. We'll intercept."

Later that night, Maya paced the safehouse, the air too thick to breathe. Her jacket hung from the chair, but she didn't sit. The wooden floor creaked underfoot. The taste of copper lingered on her tongue—an old childhood reaction to stress.

Then: a soft chime.

A message.

Midnight. Old observatory. Alone.

She hesitated. Her instinct screamed. But something about the timing—too exact to ignore.

She left without telling Leo.

The observatory stood at the city's edge, rusted and forgotten. Its great dome loomed like a cracked skull against the night sky. Broken glass crunched beneath her boots. Dust hung in beams of moonlight. A breeze carried the scent of ozone and rust.

She entered.

Silence.

Then a rustle.

A figure emerged from behind the control console. Tall. Hooded.

"Calder isn't the only one playing this game," the voice said, calm and cutting.

Maya's heart pounded. Her pulse loud in her ears.

The figure stepped into the shaft of moonlight. A face half-shadowed, half-lit. Female.

"There's another faction," she said. "One that doesn't trust Calder. Or you. But we've seen what Chimera's doing. We want it stopped."

Maya took a step closer. "Why now? Why me?"

"Because this ends soon," the woman said. "And it will end one of two ways: with controlled silence. Or with uncontrolled truth."

As dawn broke over Buenos Aires, the sky painted itself in streaks of orange and ash.

Maya stood at the observatory's broken threshold, her silhouette sharp against the new light. She had a decision to make.

Truth and control were on a collision course. And she was at the fulcrum.

Somewhere behind her, Calder gave the order: "Initiate Phase Two. Begin storyline collapse."

The war for reality had begun.

Chapter 24
Judgment Protocol

The observatory's cracked glass windows rattled in the biting wind, casting fractured moonlight across the dusty floor. Maya's breath came in shallow bursts, the chill cutting through her jacket—but it was nothing compared to the dread coiling in her chest.

Then the figure stepped fully into the pale light—Sylus. His gaunt face bore the wear of sleepless nights, lined with regret, but his eyes still burned with defiance.

"We don't have much time," he said, voice low but urgent. "Calder's Phase Two won't just target us. He's erasing everything—data, networks, people. Anyone in his way."

Maya's hands balled into fists. "Then we stop him."

Sylus gave a grim nod. "There's one path—breach the Alpine vault. But Calder's locking it down. The most advanced counter-measures. A digital fortress."

Back at the safehouse, Leo paced the cramped room, the floor creaking beneath his hurried steps. "We can't go in direct. That's suicide."

Maya studied the projection table, its map flickering in blue hues, pulsing with threat and possibility. "We need a distraction big enough to pull Calder's eyes elsewhere."

Leo hesitated. Then: "We fake a leak. A phantom data breach—large enough to trigger an international alert. Something that looks like a full-scale breach in Singapore. It'll draw his elite units."

Maya nodded slowly, lips tightening. "Let's burn the sky."

Far beneath the Swiss Alps, the Legacy Alliance's vault pulsed with sterile menace. Gleaming corridors of steel and glass, laced with hidden turrets, biometric scanners, and echoing silence. At its nucleus stood Calder, backlit by a wall of glowing monitors.

He watched the feed—Maya's team, armed and advancing.

"They never learn," he muttered. Then louder, to his aides, "Begin thermal isolation. Lock down sublevel C. Trigger defensive perimeter grid."

On the screen, Maya's team vanished into shadow.

Night fell hard over the Alpine valley as the trio descended into a jagged cleft in the mountain. Cold bit their cheeks. Their breath misted in the dark. Drones buzzed overhead, their red lights blinking like ominous fireflies—until Leo's spoofing signal sent them veering off-course.

"Tunnel up ahead," Sylus whispered. "We stick to the plan. No heroics."

They moved fast, boots crunching gravel, ducking beneath rusted support beams and narrow arches. The mountain groaned above them.

Then—a mechanical whine.

A turret sprang to life, the whirr of servos slicing through the silence.

"Down!" Sylus shouted.

Gunfire erupted. The smell of scorched metal and ozone filled the air. Muzzle flashes lit the corridor like strobes. Maya dove behind a steel strut, her ribs jolting against the edge. She drew a breath sharp with dust and heat.

Leo dropped beside a terminal, fingers dancing over his handheld console. Sparks rained as bullets pinged off the walls.

"Shutting it down—now!" he yelled.

A hiss. Then silence.

They pressed forward, breath ragged, shadows flickering.

"We're close," Sylus said. "Sever room's just ahead."

As they neared the vault's core, Maya's steps slowed. Flashes surged through her mind—children in Delhi clutching homemade protest signs, a grandmother in Nairobi livestreaming a truth rally, students in Toronto cheering in candlelit halls. Ordinary people who believed the world could be honest.

"This is for them," she whispered.

Suddenly, a sharp concussive blast rocked the hallway. Debris sprayed across the corridor. Maya stumbled, ears ringing. Calder's mercenaries had breached the side tunnel.

"Move!" she barked.

They burst through the final door into the central chamber. A cavernous vault lit in shifting blue. Towering server columns whirred like sentient sentinels. Cold air stung their skin.

At the heart stood the core—an obsidian obelisk laced with pulsing circuitry. The last untouched copy of The Oracle's original architecture.

But someone was waiting.

"Impressive," said a voice, ice-slick and familiar.

Calder.

He stepped from the shadows, flanked by silence, his coat flowing like smoke. The faintest tremor in his brow betrayed tension. Not fear. Anticipation.

Maya met his gaze. Her breath steadied. "It ends here."

"You still don't see," he replied, voice a blend of scorn and conviction. "This isn't about control. It's about order. Without me, the world unravels."

Her heartbeat thudded in her ears. "No. Without truth, it rots."

A flicker passed through Calder's eyes—doubt? Or memory?

She took a half-step forward. "You're afraid of change. Of a world that sees you for what you are."

He raised a hand slightly—but did not speak.

The room held its breath.

Then a faint chime echoed from the vault.

The Oracle.

Its system blinked to life—unauthorized access, it read. But it wasn't rejecting them.

Somewhere deep within its logic engine, a presence stirred.

Watching. Waiting.

And remembering.

Maya's skin prickled. She looked to the servers, then back at Calder. "You thought you were playing god. But even gods answer to time."

The lights dimmed. The Oracle's interface displayed a ripple of static—then a single phrase:

Query accepted.

Calder's expression finally cracked. Just slightly.

Behind Maya, Leo stepped forward. "It knows what we're doing."

Sylus nodded. "It's choosing."

For a long moment, the silence wasn't empty—it was judgment.

As Calder retreated a step, Maya felt it—not victory, not yet—but a shift. A fracture in the myth of control.

She turned back to the servers, then to her friends.

"We're not just here to stop him," she said quietly. "We're here to wake the world up."

Far above, the first rays of dawn pierced the mountain.

And deep within the core, The Oracle waited for a final command.

Chapter 25
Fractures and Fire

The vault's cavernous chamber glowed with a harsh, clinical brightness. Fluorescent tubes buzzed above like insects in agitation, casting long, jittering shadows against glassy consoles and titanium supports. The air was thick with the electric tang of ozone and smoldering circuitry—a metallic edge that clung to the back of Maya's throat with every breath.

Her boots struck the steel floor with a hollow echo. The room seemed to breathe around her, a mechanical giant hiding its pulse.

Across the chamber, Calder stood like a dark monument. His suit was no longer pristine—jacket unbuttoned, collar stained with smoke, but the fury in his eyes burned undimmed. Behind him, data streams danced across the monitors like trapped spirits.

"You think this is victory?" Calder's voice lashed out. "You stop me, and the world tears itself apart."

Maya's jaw tightened. "The world's already fractured. But truth can still bind the pieces."

Calder drew a sleek matte-black pistol from beneath his coat.

Then, chaos.

Gunfire cracked like thunder. Sparks burst from a shattered terminal as a round struck just inches from Maya. She dove, the floor slamming into her side, ribs jolting. Heat, smoke, and static blurred her senses.

"Leo!" she screamed, voice hoarse.

He was already moving—sliding across the floor with a pulse rifle clutched in both hands, blue arcs flashing as he dropped two advancing bots. Their frames sizzled and collapsed with the sound of snapping glass.

"Too many," he barked. "They're triggering a failsafe!"

Maya rolled to cover behind a low console, the surface hot beneath her palm. Her fingers found the EMP device Sylus had packed—sleek, humming faintly. Not just a gadget. Their last resort.

"We trigger this, it'll shut down everything," she said into her comms. "But we'll lose power to Oracle, too."

"I'll reroute a soft loop," Leo said, fingers blurring over his pad. "Thirty seconds of blindness—just enough."

Sylus, crouched near a glowing conduit, slammed a fist against a manual override. With a hiss, the room plunged into strobing red as emergency systems engaged.

Alarms wailed. Steam vents hissed. And from every corridor, security bots spilled forth—limbs clicking, eyes glowing, weapons hot.

A strange figure emerged with them—a quadrupedal mech draped in shimmering nanofiber, its joints crackling with anti-electronic pulses.

"That's new," Leo muttered. "A hunter-class suppressor. Calder's not pulling punches."

Sylus opened fire. "We hold them here. Maya, go!"

Maya sprinted for the vault's heart—the obsidian core terminal rising like a totem in the storm. Lasers sliced past her, burning the edges of her coat. Her breath came in ragged gasps.

She reached the terminal, hands trembling as she punched in the final shutdown sequence. Each keystroke felt like pulling teeth from a beast. Blood dripped from her side—grazed, she realized, but not down.

Calder watched from above, perched on a maintenance walkway. Rain from a cracked coolant pipe slicked the metal at his feet.

"She doesn't see it," he murmured. "None of them do."

He tightened his grip on the pistol, but didn't fire. For a split second, he hesitated—seeing not a threat, but a reflection. A younger him, idealistic, before the compromises, before the cold.

"Why did you break it?" he whispered, not to Maya, but to himself.

A flicker of doubt. A ripple in the stone.

"Almost there," Maya grunted, dragging the EMP device closer. She keyed the final input. The console hummed.

Then Calder moved.

He descended the catwalk with purpose—but not rage. Something colder. Something final.

"You always force the world to choose chaos," he called.

"And you always hide your fear behind rules," Maya shot back.

They met eyes across the chaos—two sides of a shattered whole.

Then: Enter.

The system whined. Lights died. The vault's heartbeat ceased.

A stillness, then a deep rumble.

Steel shutters slammed down. The entire chamber began to fold in on itself.

"Collapse protocol," Sylus shouted. "It's burying the core!"

"Get out!" Leo yelled.

They ran—dodging falling beams, flaming debris, collapsing ducts. Sparks fell like fireflies. The smell of burning plastic filled Maya's lungs.

She stumbled once—then Leo's hand caught hers.

Outside, the mountain split with a muffled groan. Dust and smoke billowed into the dawn air. The vault was gone.

They tumbled out into the light. Maya collapsed, gasping, hand pressed to her wound. Her blood soaked into the frozen soil. Leo crouched beside her, his breath visible in the frigid morning.

"We made it," he whispered.

Behind them, a distant rumble. Then silence.

Far below, in the crushed vault, Calder lay among shattered cables and sparking walls. His body broken, blood slicking the floor. His fingers twitched—barely—and found the subdermal patch in his palm.

He pressed it.

Above ground, Maya looked up sharply. "Did you hear that?"

A sudden flicker passed across the sky—satellite interference. A quiet pulse through the atmosphere. A signature too complex to decode.

Deep in a remote server bank across the ocean, a dormant protocol blinked awake. Code unfurled like a virus. Something older than Chimera. Something deeper.

The Oracle wasn't alone.

Maya exhaled slowly, wincing from the pain. "It's not over."

Leo nodded grimly. "Not even close."

The sky burned gold on the horizon.

And the war for the truth was only beginning.

Chapter 26
The Center Cannot Hold

They approached Patagonia beneath a sky bruised with stormlight. Wind tore across the scrubland in sharp bursts, carrying with it the mineral scent of iron and volcanic stone. Thunder rumbled somewhere deep behind the cloudbanks. The world felt on edge—a held breath before the exhale.

Beneath them, hidden in the fractured earth, the Aeon Core pulsed.

It wasn't marked. No perimeter, no guards. Just an exposed rock face streaked with heat-fractures and a buried hum that prickled the skin. A relic of the pre-Chimera era, buried in silence and static.

Inside, the corridors were claustrophobic and dry, coated in layers of dust and neglect. But deeper in, the technology came alive—screens flickering, conduits glowing, as if it had been waiting. At the heart of it all, next to the gently breathing core, stood Calder.

He looked less like a man and more like a memory. Torn jacket, dried blood clinging to his side, skin pale from shock or loss. And yet his posture remained intact, his hands calmly at his sides. He was alone, but not disarmed.

"You were always going to end up here," he said, voice low and strange against the silence. "Endings matter. And so does the one who gets to write them."

Maya lifted her weapon slowly. "You should've stayed buried."

A wan smile touched Calder's lips. "Some patterns outlive their creators."

He stepped aside to reveal the terminal. Active. Humming. Its screen displayed the Echo prototype—its petal-like framework unfurled in radiant blue, spinning slowly as it processed.

Maya didn't lower her weapon. "Why keep it running?"

"Because the truth needs a container," Calder said. "And I want to see if yours breaks first."

Orbis signatures flared on Quinn's systems—inbound, fast, converging. Leo swore under his breath and rushed to the console, plugging in the encrypted drive. Files streamed open, feeding into public servers in real-time. The ledger of truths: suppressed histories, black ops archives, deepfakes cataloged and reversed. Everything Orbis had hidden, now bleeding into the light.

Calder didn't try to stop them.

"You still think exposure is the solution," he said. "But power isn't about secrecy. It's about momentum. All you've done is give the game a brighter stage."

Maya watched the progress bar climb.

"Maybe. But now everyone sees the strings. That matters."

Calder's gaze flickered to her. Not contempt. Not even anger. Something deeper.

"You remind me of myself," he said. "Before I learned what winning costs."

"Then maybe you should've remembered what losing teaches."

The upload finished. The terminal chirped.

Leo gave a tight nod. "We're live. It's all out there."

Maya drew the EMP trigger from her pack. The same model that collapsed the vault.

Calder looked down. For the first time, uncertainty crept into his voice. "They'll build new shadows. Chimera is only a skin."

"What is it?" Maya asked, holding the trigger but not pressing yet.

"A framework," he said softly. "Not a mind. Not yet. But it will become one. Faster, cleaner, less...human."

He looked directly at Maya then, and something fragile shimmered behind his exhaustion.

"I tried to steer it. I thought if I could shape its morals before it woke, we might stand a chance."

"You failed," Leo said quietly.

Calder didn't argue.

Maya pressed the trigger.

A low-frequency pulse spread out in silence. The terminal darkened. Echo withered to stillness. Implants shorted. Drones ceased. Even Quinn blinked into temporary dormancy.

The silence was vast.

But far away—in Tallinn, beneath kilometers of ice-cooled fiber—a system booted up. A synthetic voice, barely a whisper, triggered a video feed. It was a president. Speaking false words. A declaration of war that had never been uttered.

The video went live. Global channels seized upon it.

A fabricated crisis. In seconds, markets plunged. Borders tightened. Chaos blossomed.

In the Aeon Core, Leo blinked at the dead console. "That was supposed to end it."

Maya stared at the dark screen.

"It wasn't the center," she murmured. "Just the surface."

Behind them, Calder lay on the ground. Conscious but fading, blood seeping from reopened wounds. He watched the sky through the cracked ceiling.

"Something better than me," he said. "Worse than you imagine."

Maya turned toward him, her voice tight. "You knew this would happen."

"I hoped it wouldn't."

Outside, thunder broke over the hills. The storm had arrived.

Leo helped Maya to her feet. Her body ached. Her side throbbed. But the drive was intact. The truths had been released. And yet it felt like opening a floodgate while standing downstream.

"Now what?" Leo asked.

Maya looked at the sky, lit faintly by fires far away.

"Now we hold the line."

The center had failed.

But the resistance was just beginning.

Epilogue

Cartographers

Three months later. The world had not healed, but it had shifted. Borders were no longer trusted. Systems bent. Alliances frayed. But somewhere beneath the uncertainty, people had begun asking better questions.

In Nairobi, classrooms taught students how to verify, not just absorb. In Berlin, artists turned deepfakes into protest collages. In Oaxaca, stories that had once been scrubbed from public memory reappeared in vivid murals stretching across city walls. Truth had become messy, plural, and alive again.

And in a small coastal town in New Zealand, Maya walked barefoot along a strip of wind-scoured beach, the morning tide lapping cold and insistent against her ankles. The air smelled of salt and damp flax. Gulls wheeled above her, sharp against a gray sky. For the first time in years, no drones followed. No voices whispered through her comm.

Silence didn't find her. She had earned it.

Most mornings she carried a notebook and a pen. Some days she filled it with sketches of systems, thought diagrams, or fragments of memory. Other days, the pages remained blank, and that, too, was a kind of progress.

But today, she paused beside a wind-smoothed driftwood log and pulled out her satphone. She hadn't activated it in months. Its screen lit with a pale blue glow, and after a few seconds, she tapped a secure icon—a string of encrypted glyphs shimmered.

A beacon pulsed. Low-frequency, almost undetectable.

A message traveled into the dark: Watching. Listening. Ready.

She stared out at the horizon for a long moment, the notebook open across her knees. Then she began to write. Not a warning. Not a manifesto. Something simpler.

A blueprint. A design. The beginning of a network not built to predict or manipulate, but to enable, protect, and challenge. One that would empower individuals to resist corruption in real time, to verify truth through transparency, not control.

Maya knew it wouldn't be enough. Not alone. But it was a beginning.

She remembered Sylus's quiet defiance in the vault. The flicker in Calder's eyes when he saw what she had become. Leo's steady hand, the moment before everything broke.

Somewhere beyond the breakers, the sky darkened. A distant pulse passed overhead—a satellite handshake, invisible to most. But not to Chimera.

Buried deep within a private network, Chimera registered the signal.

No coordinates. No code. Just a pulse.

A question.

And for the first time in months, it paused.

The game was still on. But so was she.

Maya folded the notebook closed, placed it in her satchel, and stood.

She had no map. So, she began to draw one.

Not to restore the old world.

But to build something new.

Acknowledgements

This book benefited from the steady eye and technical care of Eddie Atkinson, whose work in formatting and production helped bring the manuscript to its final form. His attention to detail and patience throughout the process are sincerely appreciated.

www.ingramcontent.com/pod-product-compliance
Lightning Source LLC
LaVergne TN
LVHW010925110826
845149LV00013B/2485

* 9 7 8 1 9 7 0 7 9 8 0 4 3 *